CHAS WILLIAMSON

The Seeking Series

SEEKING
Forever

ISBN 13: 978-1-945670-47-3
ISBN-10: 1-945670-47-9

Year of the Book
135 Glen Avenue
Glen Rock, PA 17327

Dedication

This book is dedicated to my partner, my soulmate, my best friend, my wife. Thank you for being there and encouraging me, for sharing all of our adventures. No heroine I could ever dream up could be as wonderful as you.

Acknowledgments

To God, for giving me such a wild and vivid imagination and for making my dreams come true.

To Janet, for taking care of all the little details, so 'all I have to do is write.'

To my family for their support and understanding.

To Travis, our guru for all things technical.

To my beta readers – Sarah, Jackie, Mary, Wendy and Connie, for your comments, corrections and advice.

To Demi, for all of her assistance in helping the original manuscript become *Seeking Forever*.

Chapter 1

*A*s the sun sank low over the waters of Lake Michigan, Kaitlin sat all alone on an iron bench on Navy Pier. With the heel of her hand, she smeared her eye shadow around her face, wiping her hands on her pants. Sniffling, she pulled the pack of Virginia Slims from her purse. With shaking hands, she lit her first cigarette since her sophomore year in college. The acrid smoke attacked her lungs as she inhaled, immediately resulting in a series of violent coughs. *God, I hate these things.*

One good thing about it, the hacking took her mind off of him. Her coughing slowly subsided. *I'm so stupid. Every time I love someone, I'm the one who gets hurt.* She watched a young couple walk by, hand in hand. *A few days ago, that was us, before he...* She shook her head as they walked away. "I am such a fool. Why in the world did I ever allow him to do this to me?"

Hating the taste of the cigarette, she flicked it into Lake Michigan, only to instinctively light up a second one. *Damn you, Jeremy. I wish I never would have met you!* Fighting back a new outburst, she said out loud, "I wish... I wish you were never born!" Their love had seemed so perfect, like a fairy tale come true. Until today.

She'd wanted to surprise him by returning to Chicago ahead of schedule. The look on Jeremy's face when she walked in certainly did show surprise, but not like she had hoped. *Damn you, Jeremy! You used me, just like every man from my past.* She blew her nose, trying to pull herself back together. *I hate you.*

She was wiping her eyes when a shadow blocked the evening sun. Standing before her was Jeremy, panting hard. His eyes were red. *Tears of regret from getting caught, huh?*

He grimaced in pain as he knelt down to look into her eyes. "Katie, I've been searching for you all afternoon. Thank God, I found you! We need to talk. It wasn't what you think! I need to explain. Will you listen to me, please?"

Her hazel eyes blazed with anger. "Are you an idiot, Jeremy? Why would I ever listen to you again?" Her fists clenched in rage. She paused long enough to catch her breath. "You were supposed to be getting better to come back to me. I will never forgive you or forget what you did!"

Quickly standing up, she tried to walk away from him. She knew he was going to lie his way out of this to try and win her back. As suspected, Jeremy grabbed her arm, turning her toward him. She wasn't really prepared to see him again, so soon after his betrayal.

His dirty-blond hair was blowing in the breeze. The dazzling brightness of his electric blue eyes revealed pain. *You certainly are a good actor, aren't you?* Her vision blurred as she studied his eyes. The same ones she had gazed into for countless hours while she nursed him back to health. The eyes that smiled at her like they did when they made love. Even now, they still sent an electric shock of desire up her spine.

Stop it! I want you out of my life! The problem was, no matter what he had done, she loved him. She always would, but she needed to get away, right now. *You may be bigger and stronger, but...* She kicked his broken leg as hard as she could.

He yelped, grabbing his wounded leg and pitching forward to the ground.

Towering over him, she yelled, "Are you hurting, Jeremy? Good! Imagine how I felt!"

He grimaced, bracing himself on the bench to stand. Then he reached out to brush the long dark hair from her eyes.

Kaitlin pulled back sharply, anger welling in her soul. "How dare you touch me after what you did!" She slapped his face as hard as she could.

He didn't try to stop her.

Pointing a finger at his face she said, "I told you I never want to see you again and I meant it!"

Ignoring what she had said, Jeremy tried to pull her close. She struggled, but was no match for his strength. Pulling her body tightly against his, he whispered, "Katie, please! I love you, only you! Please let me explain. At least hear me out."

She struggled, realizing she couldn't break free.

Out of the corner of her eye, she spotted a police officer walking nearby. He appeared to be watching them with concerned interest. *I need to get away.* "Help me, please!" she screamed. "This man is hurting me and won't let me go! Help! Please help me!"

That did it. The officer ran over to her aid, grabbing Jeremy by the arm.

Without turning from her, Jeremy slammed an elbow into the man's face, knocking him to the ground, blood spurting from his nose.

Kaitlin pulled free, racing toward the parking lot.

Jeremy started to hobble after her, but a second officer appeared out of nowhere, tackling Jeremy.

She chanced one final glance to see the three of them wrestling on the ground as she fled.

Her hands were shaky as she fumbled through her purse, searching for the car keys. Finally finding them, she started to drive. Blending into traffic, she drove around until she found herself at Warbler's Overlook. *He's gone from my life, forever.* She was so sad, she couldn't hold it in any more. Kaitlin Jenkins allowed the few remaining tears she'd held back during the day to come out. All alone in the evening dusk.

Chapter 2

(Four Months Prior)

*J*eremy shivered in the cold biting winds of early March as he entered the old Sears Tower building. He took a few deep breaths to steady his mind as the elevator ascended to the 23rd floor. *I'll have to get used to this new 'uniform.'* This would be his first post-military job. The elevator doors opened to Global Development Consultants—GDC—his new employer. After a quick survey of the area, he checked in with the receptionist.

"Welcome, Mr. Roberts. You're quite early. Please help yourself to coffee while you wait." She pointed to a Keurig in the corner.

Forty minutes precisely. Punctuality is a virtue. As Jeremy brewed his cup, he noticed the receptionist was watching him with keen interest. *Forget it, lady. You don't want anything to do with me.* Photo frames on her desk had revealed three children, but no man. *Once upon a time, I wanted a son, but that will never happen. Not anymore.*

Jeremy cursed his momentary distraction. He'd missed the opening of the elevator doors. The sudden swish of her long dress jerked his mind back to reality. Her back was to him— dark brown, shoulder-length silky hair, about five four, maybe a hundred ten or fifteen pounds. Her fingers were long and curvy. The faceless girl struck up a conversation with the receptionist. Her voice was like a wind chime in a light breeze. Some joke was shared and her laugh reminded him of someone he had once loved with all his heart. *Mom*. Jeremy wished she would turn around so he could see if she was as pretty as her voice.

The elevator chime sounded again and several men stepped out. One of them called, "Kaitlin?" She turned toward him, giving Jeremy a brief profile view. Very nice, but still he craved the complete three-sixty. His mind wandered, wondering if he would ever meet her. *Like she could ever care for me.* He wasn't suave or debonair. He wasn't attractive or witty. And even if he was, his other traits would surely drive her away.

The alarm on the woman's phone went off. "Meeting in fifteen minutes. I don't want to be late." She waved to the receptionist and scurried off. Jeremy realized his palms were sweaty.

He checked his watch—fifteen minutes to go. He made good use of his time, replaying the mission in his head. *Mission? At least no one will try to kill me on this assignment. Hopefully.*

Quickly opening his laptop, he re-read the project description, although it was already committed to memory. He would be doing recon for a client to help them choose a location for a new facility. The client had a reputation for attracting and retaining the best employees, so they wanted to assure their new location would provide all the amenities that highly talented people might desire.

To accomplish this, GDC was sending in two "scouts"—a gentleman named Trent Laughman, and

Jeremy. He had met Laughman briefly during the interview process. A former U.S. Marshall, the man was quiet and no-nonsense, just the type of partner Jeremy preferred.

Precisely at 2:00 P.M., the receptionist led Jeremy to a large conference room with an oversized, ornate mahogany table. From the windows, the view of Lake Michigan was breathtaking.

A tall, muscular man rose to greet him. Jeremy had met the CEO, John Stange, several times during the interview process. He appeared to be strict but fair, traits Jeremy could respect. Stange introduced him to the eight people sitting around the table. Jeremy stood in perfect military posture, giving each full attention with a firm handshake and a proper 'sir' or 'ma'am' greeting.

Finally, Stange lifted a hand toward the last remaining attendee. "This is Kaitlin Jenkins, Assistant Operations Manager for the Midwest. She will be accompanying you on your journey. Trent Laughman had a family emergency."

As soon as he saw her, Jeremy recognized the girl from the lobby. Now that he could see her from a full frontal position, he could properly assess her looks. *I wouldn't mind seeing her face every day... say for the rest of my life!*

Jeremy turned to Stange without saying hello. "I'm sorry. Did you say Mr. Laughman was not able to participate in this mission?"

Stange eyed him strangely, "That's correct. Kaitlin is the best of the best in this company. And son, you aren't in the Rangers anymore. It's not a mission, it's a project." His brows furrowed as he measured Jeremy. "Is there going to be a problem working with Kaitlin?"

Great! I'm already screwing this up. "No, sir. I just wanted to make sure I heard you correctly." To Kaitlin, he bowed slightly. "It is an honor to be assigned to this project with you, Ms. Jenkins." He extended a hand, hoping his embarrassment didn't show.

The look she gave him revealed as much enthusiasm as if she had received notice the IRS was auditing her taxes. All that changed when her hand touched his. A zap of static electricity shocked them both. Jeremy expected she would retract her hand, but instead she grasped it tightly in return, staring confidently back at him. Those hazel eyes made it clear she was assessing him. "Likewise, Mr. Roberts, likewise."

Jeremy was disappointed when the handshake ended. For the rest of the meeting, he would remember the softness of her skin. As she sat down, the look of confidence in her eyes was replaced with something else, but he couldn't name exactly what it was.

Stange ran through his presentation, but Jeremy found it hard to concentrate. While avoiding direct eye contact with Kaitlin, he glanced her way. Each time, she was also watching him. Worry began to build in his mind. Stange had told him it would be a five day a week project that would last for six months. *How will I be able to function for six months with her?* He would have to guard himself closely.

The meeting wound down with Stange finalizing the schedule and expectations. After everyone left, Jeremy waited to speak with Kaitlin. She was engrossed with her tablet, but turned pale when she noted him standing there. Quickly, she stuffed the device into her bag.

Again, Jeremy politely extended his hand, "Ms. Jenkins, I was wondering if you might want to get acquainted over a cup of coffee or some dinner." The look she flashed was like he'd asked her to jump into a volcano. "I mean," Jeremy hedged, "since we're going to be working together for half a year."

It seemed she had already made her mind up before the words left his lips. Her reply was swift, "I'm not looking for a new BFF. I believe John gave you the keys to the rental car, so I'll meet you here at noon Sunday. We can drive straight to the first site from here."

Jeremy didn't show any emotion. *Talk about making friends and influencing people!* "All right, Ms. Jenkins, if that's what you prefer. But it might be easier if I picked you up at home." *That sounded wrong.* "I mean so you don't have to drag luggage downtown." He jotted something down and handed her a slip of paper. "This is my cell number. In case you change your mind. Otherwise, I'll meet you in front of the building Sunday at twelve hundred hours sharp."

He nodded, turned quickly on his heels and rapidly walked to the elevator. He didn't know why, but he felt something very important had just happened. *Yeah, like me making an enormous fool of myself.* Walking out into the snow flurries at street level, his thoughts were on the pretty girl he had met—Kaitlin. Despite his past, could it be that he was finally ready to open his heart and soul to someone? He could hardly wait for noon on Sunday to find out.

Chapter 3

Kaitlin stood in front of the Tower, surrounded by six bags of luggage. Once again, she reviewed the checklist she'd created. It had cost a fortune to have a cab drop her off downtown, but she couldn't have handled this much luggage on the Metro. It would have been simpler to accept Roberts' offer to pick her up at home, but after the way she'd treated him...

That wasn't the only reason for her stubbornness, though.

The determining factor had been the absolutely stupid doodling he'd caught her doing on her tablet. When the meeting ended, she turned to find that damned Roberts standing right behind her. *Did he see what I wrote?* No, he would have said something, wouldn't he? Kaitlin knew she had to put those kind of feelings away. She did not want to be hurt, *again!* That was the real reason she had not called him.

At precisely twelve o'clock, a black Suburban pulled along the curb in front of her. Out stepped Jeremy. Dressed in clean, worn jeans and a dark blue fleece jacket, his short dirty-blond hair blew in the breeze. Electric blue eyes blazed a path directly into her heart, her soul.

He simply nodded, "Good afternoon, Ms. Jenkins."

Grabbing two pieces of luggage in each hand, he swiftly walked to the rear of the SUV. Lowering the bike rack so he could open the tail gate, he had them loaded while she struggled just to pull the other two roller bags to the rear of the vehicle. He met her halfway, taking the gear from her. She followed, noticing he had only packed one large duffel bag.

She turned to him. "What's with the bike?"

When he smiled, she saw how his eyes also smiled at her. *Cute!*

"My objectives for this mission, I mean project, require boots on the ground recon. The bike will be the best way to get around."

She raised her eyebrows at his explanation. She hadn't thought of that. "Don't you think it would have been nice to ask if I wanted to bring my bike along, too?" *If I owned one.*

His smile vanished. "Probably, but I didn't have your cell number. Do you want to swing around and pick yours up?"

"It's a little late for that. We have a long drive. From now on, I expect better communication."

"I'm sorry. I will do better next time, Ms. Jenkins."

This trip was going to be difficult enough without being adversarial from the first step. She frowned. "I think we got off on the wrong foot. Please call me Kaitlin, okay?"

He gave her an easygoing smile. "All right, Ms. Jenkins. If you would prefer, I will call you Kaitlin, and you may call me Jeremy."

"Didn't you bring any luggage, Jeremy?"

He laughed. "It seems you and I have different methods of packing, that's all." He walked to the passenger door and held it open for her. "After you, ma'am."

Kaitlin slid in and he closed the door. As she latched her seat belt, she tried to remember the last time a man had held a door for her. His politeness unnerved her. Her stomach clenched as she fought the urge to drop her defenses.

The miles slid by silently until the quiet became irritating. "Look, can we call a truce? I didn't intend to be mean the other day. It's... well... work is work and private is private. I don't want to blend the two."

Jeremy was silent for a moment. "Yes ma'am, I can understand that. I wasn't trying to hit on you or flirt with you. But I was an Army Ranger and I believe that you have to trust those you work with, otherwise it's going to be a long six months."

"Army Ranger!" Kaitlin's great grandfather had been a Ranger in World War II. And every day for the rest of his life.

He nodded without taking his eyes off the road. "What brought you to GDC?" he asked.

"I graduated from Northwestern University and worked in a couple of accounting firms. I want to become a senior manager, and I'm hoping this assignment is what will get me there." Kaitlin shocked herself. She never revealed so much, especially to strangers. But suddenly, there was so much more she wanted to share. "So, now we know each other," she said to stop herself before revealing any more details.

"Yes ma'am, I guess we do."

"Any chance you can quit calling me ma'am? I'm not that old!"

His eyes crinkled as he laughed. "It has nothing to do with your age. It's all about respect."

Respect? Kaitlin simply nodded her head and watched the guard rails slip by. From time to time, she would steal a quick look at him, taking in his aura, but when he glanced back, she would swiftly look away.

Despite her heart's attraction to Jeremy, the closeness alarm warned her to be careful. She didn't know him, but he was a man. And that never turned out good.

Kaitlin's mind wrestled the battle from her heart. She plugged in her headphones and leaned against the window.

Jeremy tuned in a Country music station and considerately turned the volume low.

Those bulging Ranger muscles couldn't be hidden by a fleece jacket. The questions in her heart were many, but instead of asking them, Kaitlin obeyed her mind and remained silent.

Chapter 4

*J*eremy hesitated before waking her. She looked like an angel perched in the passenger seat. "We're here," he said, gently shaking her arm.

'Here' was their first stop, a moderate-sized city in western Ohio. To avoid bias, they'd decided to refer to the stops only as letters. At Town A's motel, he found a cart and loaded Kaitlin's collection of luggage.

She held up a finger to signal him to wait because she was texting on her phone.

His mind drifted. Even though they had barely spoken, Jeremy found himself attracted to this beautiful girl. As always, he paid attention to the tiniest detail, spending his afternoon watching her mannerisms and listening to the few words she had spoken. He concluded she was either in a long-term romance or had been badly hurt. She wasn't wearing a ring, yet he couldn't comprehend how any man would not want to make a commitment to her. He feared something horrible must have happened in her past to make her guard her inner self the way she did.

He thought they'd made a connection when they stopped for dinner, but then again, maybe it was all in his mind. *Doesn't matter anyway. She's way out of my league.*

Kaitlin continued to text while he waited.

She wasn't the kind of woman Jeremy had known in his past. Okay, the only girl he had ever been with was Britany. That romance had ended quickly—eight months after their marriage began.

He shook his head as he contemplated why.

Six weeks after they'd said 'I do,' he'd volunteered for another tour of duty in Iraq. With disgust, he remembered the look on her face when he told her. He probably should have discussed it with her first, but then Britany probably should have mentioned that she needed more than one man in her life to satisfy her needs.

Jeremy felt eyes on him. He glanced up to catch her questioning gaze.

"Are you all right?" Kaitlin asked. "You look like you're going to be sick. Didn't dinner agree with you?"

"No, ma'am," he said. "Just remembering something that left a bitter taste. Can I give you a hand with your luggage?"

She smiled. "That would be nice, but only on one condition."

Jeremy's spirits raised a little. "Okay, what's that?"

"Quit calling me ma'am. I told you it makes me feel old," she scoffed. "I sure hope you listen better in the future than what you have today, or we're going to have a serious problem."

He quickly straightened. "No, ma-... I mean, no, Ms. Jenkins. It won't happen again."

Her eyes flashed with anger as they met his, but he wasn't sure if it was at him or something else.

Kaitlin shook her head. "Don't bother helping. I'll do it myself." She grabbed the cart and tried to yank it forward. Her effort barely moved the stuffed trolley.

"What do you have in those bags, concrete blocks?" he snickered as he muscled the cart in a way he hoped made it look easy. "You could easily strain your back trying to handle this heavy load. We're going to need to work as a team on this project."

Kaitlin blushed, not meeting his eyes.

Ah ha! So maybe it's not me she's mad at.

"Whatever. Push it if you want to. I managed just fine before you showed up this afternoon." They didn't say anything else, except for checking in at reception. After standing as far away as the elevator would allow, she unlocked the door to her room.

Jeremy moved inside, checking behind the door, then in the bathroom and even the small closet. He examined the window and door locks before finally checking under the bed.

"What are you doing?" Kaitlin snapped, crossing her arms and glaring.

"Sorry, ma-... I mean, Kaitlin. I wanted to make sure the area was safe before I left. A few minutes of good recon can prevent months or years of regret." He unloaded each bag and set them in a neat line next to the wall. One glance at her annoyed posture indicated it was time to retreat to a safer location. "I wish you a good night."

Jeremy returned the cart to the front desk. *I wish you a good night?* What he really wanted to do was look into those hazel eyes, hold her beautiful hands, and thread his fingers through her long silky hair. He'd been fantasizing since Friday about what those lips would feel like on his. *Sure! The only thing those lips will do is cover the teeth after she bites my head off!* But still, he imagined what she would feel like in his arms under a full moon, to gaze into her eyes as... He snapped to attention! *Eighty-six those thoughts, Roberts. They will lead nowhere.*

Chapter 5

*J*eremy watched her walk to their table. "Morning, Kaitlin. Sleep well?"

He had a steaming hot cup of coffee waiting for her, exactly the way she liked it. It was something he had done every day for five weeks at their eight o'clock strategy session.

"What's good about it?" she grumbled.

Like most days, her hair was wet from a morning shower and she'd not yet applied her makeup. *Not that she needs it*. He didn't dare mention his thoughts because that would be a personal thing. He shot her a million-dollar smile. "Mornings are my favorite time of the day, when the world is full of promise."

"Good for you. Let's discuss our work plan."

After the meeting, they shared a breakfast table, and as usual she spent the time texting someone on her phone.

Today she didn't look up, but obviously felt his eyes on her. "Something on your mind this morning, Roberts?"

"No, sorry. How about I take the bike today and you can have the Suburban?"

"Sure. Why should today be any different?"

In the city, Jeremy felt she would be safer in the Suburban, which is why he always took the bike. Of course he couldn't tell her that.

"Then it's settled. See you at five. It's been a little warm lately, so the AC in the Suburban should keep you comfortable." *While I sweat myself silly on the bike.* "Hope you have a really great day."

She was still concentrating on her phone. "Yeah, whatever."

Every afternoon, he made sure to return early and be freshly showered before their afternoon meeting. He set out a cold bottle of water and her favorite snack of peanut butter cups for her. She always kept it in business mode, but as he shared his insights about things like neighborhood cohesiveness, gang activity, police coverage, and friendliness of the people, he warmed under her compliments.

Kaitlin spent her days researching the availability of family and social activities and other similar intangibles. They had become a great working team. Being exceedingly diligent, he suspected she spent most nights working on her reports as the senior consultant. Despite the closeness of their working relationship, Kaitlin kept Jeremy at arm's length.

Like always, as she walked to the lobby, she was concentrating on the phone in her hand.

"Afternoon," he said.

"Wait a sec." She finished keying in something before setting the phone down.

"Who are you always texting?" he wanted to ask, but didn't. *Your boyfriend?* Maybe she regretted being stuck on the road with him while the one she loved was elsewhere.

Pulling her laptop from her bag, she said, "Okay, I'm ready. Give me your report."

I missed you, too, honey. How was your day?
Jeremy pulled out his notepad, and downloaded his observations to her for the next forty-five minutes.

"Very thorough. Nice job. Anything else?" she responded coolly.

"No, that's it. Anything on your agenda tonight?"

She glared at him for a moment. "The usual. You have the easy part. All you have to do is take notes, while I'm stuck documenting everything. Just another wasted day."

"I have an idea! We could shake things up if you want. Would you like to..."

"No! Good night." Kaitlin stuffed her laptop in her bag and left.

Every night for the first week, Jeremy had asked her to dinner. And every night she came up with an excuse. *In case you care, I'm going for a bike ride, then a hike. Afterwards, I'll find a nice cliff to jump off of...*

Biking and hiking was how he killed the lonely evenings, but his thoughts usually drifted to Kaitlin instead of the beauty of nature surrounding him. Not even with Britany had he been so enchanted. Maybe it was wishful thinking, but in his mind, his observant eye told him he was missing something.

Occasionally, if he looked quickly when they travelled, he would catch her watching him. But when he did, she always turned away. He tried several times to strike up a conversation, but only received monosyllabic answers. *Perhaps I'm seeing something that isn't really there.*

He headed out to his bike for an evening ride, but his heart stayed at the motel, with the girl in room 212.

Chapter 6

Kaitlin immediately noticed something different in his eyes when they met for their evening debrief a few days later. "Something bothering you, Roberts?"

He turned to look out the window and gestured as he spoke. "I don't like this town. Lots of signs of gang activity as well as a severe lack of friendliness."

She could tell he was tense, as if something was very wrong. His observation concerned her, because he had never expressed anything like this about the other candidate cities. "What are you trying to say?"

He turned, peering into her eyes. "I don't mean to be blunt, but I'm advising you not to go anywhere in this town without me. I counted seven different gang signs, and an inordinate number of Humvees and Escalades with tinted windows. I'm also pretty sure I witnessed a drug transaction in a school zone." He pointed out the window. "Police presence is almost non-existent. And this is the first place where I saw very young hookers and their pimps out on street corners... in the daylight, mind you. I don't want you to go out tonight without having me with you."

She studied his eyes as her anger grew, finally exploding from her lips. "How dare you think you can control me! What I do in my spare time is my business, not yours. Are we clear on that?"

His face slowly turned red. "I understand that, but we're a team. I don't want anything to happen to you."

"Well, isn't that precious?" Her voice dripped with sarcasm. "Big strong Jeremy wants to protect poor little helpless Kaitlin!" Hands on her hips, she huffed, "I am fully capable of handling myself, so piss off! And quit stalking me!"

She stormed off to her room. She hadn't really been planning on going out that night, but he had forced the issue. From her luggage, she retrieved her shortest skirt and skimpiest top. *Since I'm sure you'll be watching, I want you to see me in this!*

Kaitlin drove to the mall, which wasn't that far away. A quick walk around the top floor revealed that well over half the stores were empty. Her hands felt dirty after touching the railing. Most of the windows of the bottom floor had graffiti painted on them, reminding her of the graphics she commonly saw emblazoned on rail cars. She shuddered. *Maybe Jeremy was right.* Taking the escalator down to the food court, she saw three-quarters of the restaurant spaces were empty. From a fast food stand, she ordered takeout and headed for the parking lot. She would feel better once she was back in her room, with the chain and deadbolt firmly secured.

A burst of raucous laughter behind her made her to turn to see what caused the commotion. That's when she noticed them—five men in their late teens or early twenties on the escalator close behind her. When they saw her check over her shoulder, they started trying to talk to her, making suggestive comments. "Damn girl! You got nice legs!" Frightened, she picked up the pace.

Darkness greeted her as soon as she exited the sliding doors. Only about ten percent of the parking lot lights were lit. Tendrils of fear ran up and down her spine. Glancing over her shoulder again, she saw the men were still behind her, closing the gap quickly.

They tried a different approach. "Hey lady, you dropped something."

Kaitlin was too smart to fall for their ploy. She dug her keys out of her purse, calculating how quickly she could get into the Suburban when a sudden movement to her left caught her eye.

Out of nowhere, Jeremy appeared on his bike. Hopping off, he let it slam to the ground as he stepped between Kaitlin and the men, now less than ten steps away. "You boys looking for trouble? If you are, you've found it."

She quickly flung open the car door and climbed in, breathless. Jeremy closed the gap as he walked toward the men, flexing his hands into fists. They quickly retreated to the mall.

Jeremy turned in anger. "I hope you see what I meant, now!"

Despite her relief, she growled, "Damn you! Why did you follow me?"

A lone parking lot light flickered to life, causing the electric blue of his eyes to shimmer. "I was afraid for you."

As she put on her seatbelt, she yelled, "I don't believe you! Quit stalking me! You just can't help it, can you?"

He recoiled as if she had hit him. "I told you, I was afraid for you," he said more gently.

"That's crap and you know it. You often say we're a team, yet you can't even be honest with me. What the hell? I want the truth! Why did you follow me?"

His look of defiance crumbled. Head down, he answered, "You want the truth?" Hesitating for a few seconds, he finally lifted his eyes to look into hers. "I followed you because I care about you. For more than just work."

In the dome light of the Suburban she saw his face blush red again before he shook his head and turned to walk away.

Kaitlin's mouth dropped open.

Before she could move, he spun around to return to the Suburban, pointing a finger at her face. "I have seen too many people I really, really cared about get hurt or die." Jeremy was breathing hard as he stared at her face. "If you think I will sit idly by and allow something to happen to you, you better re-think it."

Wait. *He just said he really cares for me.* Suddenly, something changed in Kaitlin's heart. She had been wrong. This wasn't about control at all. *You really do care!* She got out and took a step toward him. "Maybe I was a little harsh. Come, put your bike on the rack and I'll give you a ride back to the motel."

He backed away. "I don't think that's a good idea, ma'am. I need a ride to clear my head. See you in the morning." He promptly mounted his bicycle and rode off.

Kaitlin's mind was going five hundred miles an hour. For weeks she had pushed him away, but now? She dialed his cell, wanting to apologize again, but mainly because she needed to hear his voice. It went straight to voicemail. In all these weeks, she had never known him to make or receive a call, except with her, so obviously he was ignoring her now.

Deep in thought, Kaitlin didn't notice when she ran a stop sign. Not even the horn or squealing tires from a car that narrowly missed T-boning the Suburban interrupted her train of thought. She had thought he only acted like he did out of politeness, but that wasn't what he had said. He told her he cared for her. How had she missed this?

She almost ran a second stop sign, but the air horn from a tractor trailer made her slam on the brakes just in time. Slowly, she realized she wanted things to be different. *What would happen if I had the courage to join you for dinner?*

It wasn't only his muscular appearance that caught her interest. She was growing quite fond of the morning cup of coffee prepared exactly the way she liked it, and being pampered with her favorite snack every afternoon. "Even on days when I act like a bitch or yell at you, you are always so kind," she muttered to the steering wheel.

The way he treated her was so different from every other man she had ever known. The initial attraction had grown into a little dream she had, the fantasy of them as a couple. Suddenly, the possibility wasn't so farfetched. Was it really possible he wasn't like the other men she had known?

The driver behind her blew his horn. Looking in the mirror, Kaitlin caught a glimpse of herself, stunned by what she saw... by what was missing. Her focus shifted from her eyes to her lips. "I want more from life than what I already have. So much more," she whispered. "What do you want, Jeremy? Is it the same thing I want?"

Her chest felt funny inside as she said aloud, "At breakfast, I will apologize. I will ask if you want to be my friend. Then... then we'll see where it goes from there." She started counting the seconds until morning.

Chapter 7

*J*eremy was mad at himself. Following Kaitlin had only angered her, but he would do it again in a heartbeat if he felt she was in danger. Then he'd called her ma'am. Again. Yes, she'd certainly be pissed about that for the entire day. And worst of all, he had committed the cardinal sin. He told her how he felt. That he cared for her, a lot. *How could I have been so stupid?*

She'd had a different kind of look on her face when he'd blurted it out, but he couldn't quite read what she was thinking. Kaitlin had made it clear on numerous occasions that work was work and personal was off-limits. He hadn't meant to say anything, but when she pressed him... it sort of came out.

Now, rather than starting the day off getting lectured, he decided to skip the coffee and breakfast meeting. Kaitlin was alive, beautiful, irresistible, and full of spirit. That was all that mattered. He always seemed to bring out the worst in her. Maybe this whole civilian thing wasn't really for him. He was having serious problems coping with it. *The door to return to the Rangers is still open.*

But when the lead gunslinger can't keep up with the men under him, weakness like that puts all of them at risk. Jeremy's last mission in Afghanistan had been proof enough of that. If he...

The sudden presence of her scent stopped his train of thought. He looked up to see her standing there staring at him. Her voice brought him back to reality. With a weak but worried smile she said, "Morning. I missed our scintillating morning conversation at breakfast."

He grunted in response. *Oh, you mean you telling me exactly what each of us is going to do today?*

Jeremy watched her face, waiting for her to unload on him.

The change in her expression confused him. "Talk to me," she said. "Are you all right?"

He nodded slowly. "Just peachy," he replied, waiting for the catch.

She dropped her head, staring at the floor. With hesitation in her voice, she softly said, "I owe you an apology for the way I treated you. I overreacted. Will you accept my apology?" Her eyes engaged his as she offered her hand for him to shake.

He waited a few seconds before enveloping her hand with his. Her skin was so warm and soft. He looked away, suddenly interested in the floral designs on the carpet. "Look, I don't expect you to understand, but I can't work today. I have somewhere I need to go. Maybe we can stay tomorrow and finish up here?" He had decided to finish this town's assignment before telling her he was leaving—returning to the Rangers.

"No need for that. I agree with your assessment of this place. As far as I'm concerned, we're done here." She touched his cheek to bring his eyes up to look at her face. "May I ask where you're going? I might want to tag along."

Definitely not a good idea. Jeremy inhaled slowly to prevent choking up, "You won't want to. Today is my mother's birthday. I want to go and pay my respects."

"Oh," she paused, searching his eyes. "Of course you should be with your family, but..." her smile came out, "maybe you'd like some company?"

Jeremy ran his gaze over her face, ending up at her eyes. *I want to say no, but if I'm leaving tomorrow, this will be the last day we'll ever spend together.* He dropped his gaze. "It's up to you," he said, shrugging his shoulders.

Kaitlin shot him the prettiest smile he had ever seen. "Great! Let me go finish packing." Her whole disposition brightened as she giggled. "Swing by my room in ten? Might need help with my concrete block collection."

He nodded. Fifteen minutes later, they were driving. Storm clouds hadn't opened yet, but the darkness of the sky matched his soul. Kaitlin must have sensed his depression. For once, she wasn't texting or listening to tunes on her phone.

They were almost out of town when they passed a woman in a white dress with yellow flowers, laughing while walking hand in hand with a young boy on the sidewalk. Memories of his mother flooded Jeremy's mind. He hadn't cried in years, but sadness started to fill his heart.

He missed two light cycles before Kaitlin asked, "You sure you're doing okay?"

No way he could look at Kaitlin right now. *You would never understand.*

She softly touched his arm, allowing her fingers to linger. "It's okay if you don't want to talk. I'm here for you. Remember, you can always talk to me."

Yeah, right. He nodded.

Time slid by as he turned off the interstate, heading twenty miles down a two-lane highway. Rain started pouring as they entered Jeremy's hometown. On Oak Street, he stopped in front of a modest home with a wraparound porch. *There it is. Where my happiness once lived.* He stopped but didn't shut off the engine.

She looked at the house, turning to him with a smile. "Is this where your mom lives?"

He shook his head, "Not anymore. This is the house where I was raised. Should've seen the flowers Mom used to plant and the way she decorated for Christmas. I just wanted to see it one last time." His hands were trembling as he pulled away. He drove three miles down the road, slowly turning into a cemetery.

With wide eyes, Kaitlin suddenly understood. She whispered, "I-I-I didn't know—I didn't understand. I'm so sorry for invading your privacy. Please forgive me."

Jeremy didn't bother to answer. He parked near a beautiful stone, engraved with entwined hearts. Stepping out, he slowly shuffled to the grave he had not visited since the day he buried them. He touched the names gently. "Hi Dad. Happy sixtieth birthday, Mom." His mind drifted back and he was thirteen again, on the day when a driver had fallen asleep behind the wheel, killing his parents. Jeremy dropped to his knees, slowly losing the battle to hold back the sorrow.

He didn't know how long he was lost in thought before noticing Kaitlin behind him, her hands gently resting on his shoulders. "What happened? Please tell me," she said softly.

There in the pouring rain, he told his story. One minute he was happily goofing off in class, the next, he was burying his parents—something no thirteen year old should ever have to endure.

"The last time I saw Mom, she wanted to kiss me goodbye. I wouldn't let her because I didn't want my friends to see it. She joked with me, saying she'd let me off the hook if I told her I loved her. I refused, because I was a stupid, stupid teenager. Now, I'd give anything to tell her I love her, to have her kiss me. My happiness ended when she died." His fingers slowly traced her name on the stone.

Kaitlin dropped to her knees beside him in the rain, wrapping her arms around him tightly. She held him as his misery finally poured out. She pulled him close until his tears were exhausted.

They were both soaked to the bone. Returning to the Suburban, he opened the passenger door for her, but she protested. "Why don't I drive, if that's okay?"

Nodding, he walked around to open the driver's door for her.

He was shaking all over, not quite sure if it was from being drenched or from the stress of the day. *Why didn't I tell Mom I loved her? I wish I'd been in the car that day, too.*

His eyes were focused on the rain splattering against the windshield. Kaitlin gently touched his chin, turning his head so they could see each other's eyes. She used her thumbs to wipe away his tears. "I think you need a friend today. I really want to be that friend."

Why now, because you pity me? Jeremy stared in disbelief. He roughly said, "Don't feel obligated to do this. You said work was work, personal was personal. Being friends is personal."

She smiled shyly. "I know. Confusing, aren't I? I don't mean to be—not with you. After all, you were the one who offered friendship first. Look at last night. You could have simply let me go, especially after the way I treated you, but you didn't. I don't want to think what might have happened if... But you offered me real friendship and not just in words. Your actions proved it." Kaitlin brushed the wet locks from her face. "Let me be honest with you. I don't really have any friends, so I'm not very good at this. Can we at least try?"

Again, he could only stare. All thoughts of his problems disappeared. Jeremy slowly nodded.

Kaitlin smiled. "Good. Now, since we are friends, I want to do something nice for you today, okay?"

His heart started to rise out of the low place it had been. He didn't have any friends, either. He had some close buddies, but no one he considered to be a real friend. A tiny smile formed as he nodded once again.

She held her finger up. "But before we do anything, we need to get your mom some flowers. After all, it is her birthday. After that, we'll take a little trip, okay?"

The tiny smile grew into a larger one. "I would like that. What are you thinking?"

Her smile was now mischievous, "Oh, I can't tell you. It's a surprise!"

Chapter 8

*K*aitlin smiled at her reflection in the mirror. It had been years since she felt this hopeful, anxious, and excited. Something had changed inside her heart last night, for the first time since Ronnie in college. Longing for companionship had caused her to do something she never dreamed about doing for a man. When he made his accidental confession, the dam of loneliness had burst. On an impulse, she had made two sets of reservations.

Her stomach was full of butterflies as they placed a large bouquet of flowers on Jeremy's mother's grave. He bought something else, though she didn't see what he had in the second bag. Then they headed back through town toward the interstate.

"Thanks again for coming today. As always, you seem to know what's best."

When he became silent, she chanced a glance. He had a wolfish smile, "So, what's the surprise?"

Her smile encompassed her heart. Feelings she wanted to shout out loud were trying to get out, but she wasn't ready to completely open up, yet. "Now if I told you, it wouldn't be a surprise, would it?"

"'Kay, but can I help you navigate?"

"Nope, Siri has it all figured out."

"This is a hands-free cell state. I better hold onto your phone so you don't get a ticket."

She giggled, "So predictable! You're just trying to find out where we're going." Her laughter stopped as she glanced into his tired eyes. "Why don't you take a nap? It's gonna be a late night and you won't want to fall asleep, I promise you that."

His eyes crinkled in a smile that made her blush. "Uh, you're in a rare mood. I don't think I want to miss out on it by sleeping. Maybe we can talk?"

Her hands shook. This was exactly what she wanted! "Ever play twenty questions, Mr. Roberts?"

"No. How do you play?"

"It's simple. I ask a question, you answer, then it's your turn to ask me a question. Of course, we need some ground rules."

He laughed as he rolled his eyes. "Of course you do..."

She ignored his playful jab. "Um-hmm. First question, after your parents passed away, what happened to you? How did you end up in the Rangers?"

His sudden laugh startled her. "So, ma'am—I mean, Kaitlin—that sounds like two questions, or is this one of your ground rules? Is that how you play the game?"

She replied with a little laugh of her own, "Touché!"

He told her about living with his aunt in Michigan, and somehow managing to graduate with a master's degree in history. Then he hesitated. "My turn. Who are you always texting? I mean, you do it constantly. If you don't have any friends, who is it? Do you have a boyfriend out there somewhere?"

Talk about going for the kill! "That was three questions, so I get to pick which one I'll answer. I really do have friends; they simply happen to be my sisters and parents. We're a close-knit bunch."

"Tell me about your family."

"What gives, Jeremy Allen Roberts? I tried to slip in a free question and you shut me down, but then you try the same thing."

He laughed again. "Point well taken, Kaitlin Elizabeth Jenkins. Ask away."

Her face broke into a wide smile. *He remembered my full name!* "How did you end up in the Rangers?" He was momentarily silent. "You don't have to answer..."

His response was sobering. "Kaitlin, I need to warn you; my life was far from perfect. Some memories take a while to get out and might scare you, but I will tell you everything. I promise you that."

He drew another deep breath. "The moment I saw those planes crash into the towers, I knew I had to do something, right then. I lost friends who worked there. To me, that day was like the Japanese attack on Pearl Harbor. It changed the fabric of our nation. I had to do something, that very moment. When the second plane slammed into the tower, I left my apartment and never went back. I volunteered for the Army. They assigned me to the Rangers."

"I remember where I was when the attacks occurred. It was such a horrible day." She grew silent.

His voice surprised her, "That's in the past. Let's not let those memories darken this wonderful day. Is it my turn?" She nodded. Quietly, he asked, "Do you have a boyfriend?"

Again, he was going for the jugular. "I will answer on two conditions, okay?" She glanced to make sure he nodded. Something about the look in his eyes intrigued her. Was it hopefulness? "I will answer yes or no, but won't give any details. That's part one. Part two is you have to answer the same question. Do you agree?"

"Agreed."

"No, I don't have a boyfriend now. Not since college. Your turn."

"No, I don't have a boyfriend now, either," Jeremy replied.

Kaitlin almost ran off the road. "Oh my God! I'm sorry. I didn't realize you were gay."

He broke into laughter so hard she thought he might hit his head on the dash. "You are so gullible!"

"What?" Finally she'd decided to crack open the door to her love life, and it just figured that he'd be gay.

"There is not a gay bone in my body, Kaitlin. And no, I don't have a girlfriend. Not for years." When he saw she wasn't laughing, he added, "So how can someone as wonderfully perfect as you not have a boyfriend? Are you an axe murderer or something?"

Kaitlin's face blushed bright red and the distance between them seemed to vanish. She wondered if he would kiss her.

His smile slowly appeared. "I really like this game. Is it my turn again?"

She smiled, not only with her lips, but with her whole heart. *The only thing that would make this better would be if I found out you painted toenails and gave foot massages!* "No, Mr. Roberts, it's my turn."

Chapter 9

*T*he original twenty questions turned into fifty. Jeremy's mind was swirling over events of the day as they passed signs for Nashville. He had fond memories of visiting the Grand Old Opry one Saturday each month with his parents. He hadn't been back since they died.

Kaitlin's voice brought him back to awareness. "Did you run out of things to ask me? It is your turn."

Jeremy shook his head, "Sorry about that, I was lost in thought. Okey dokey, what are your favorites?"

"Favorite what?"

"Songs, color, perfume, everything. I want to know it all."

She giggled and turned off the interstate, heading down a little two-lane paved road. "That's not a fair question, so I suggest we table it until tomorrow. Or maybe the day after."

He couldn't believe how enjoyable it was talking with her. Kaitlin turned down a dusty dirt road, pulling up in front of a picturesque white clapboard colonial with pink shutters. "We're here!"

"Where exactly is *here*?" he asked, looking around at the perfectly manicured flower beds.

She shoved the transmission into park, and turned to face him. "This is a Bed and Breakfast. Part one of your surprise. You ready?"

He turned to study her face, "No, not yet."

"Why not?" Her brows furrowed. "Don't you like surprises?"

He held up a finger. "Close your eyes," he said, reaching into the backseat to retrieve a bag from the florist.

She smiled as she complied. Jeremy had to stop to admire her pretty face. *Definitely way out of my league!* He pulled a bouquet of yellow roses from the bag, placing them on the console. "You can look now, Kaitlin."

"Oh, they're beautiful!" Her eyes closed as she breathed in their fragrance. When she opened them, they were sparkling. "No one's ever given me flowers before. Well, besides my dad." She reached for him, giving him a quick hug, then pulled back to study his face.

He saw a look there he hadn't seen before. *Is it longing, or affection, or...?*

Kaitlin whispered, "Jeremy, I think I want to... I want to..." She became silent as she studied his face.

Jeremy wondered exactly what she was thinking. *What do you want?*

The smile slowly faded, only to be replaced by blushing. "I think I want to go inside now."

In less than five, they were seated in the parlor, drinking iced sweet tea and chatting with their hostess. Their hands brushed, and almost at the same time, they reached for each other. The feeling and warmth of her hand in his filled Jeremy's heart.

After moving their bags to their rooms, Kaitlin drove them to Nashville. Following dinner, she pointed the SUV onto Opryland Drive. With a wide smile, he asked, "Does the second part of the surprise involve the Grand Old Opry?"

Her eyes were full of stars as she handed him the print-out of who would be on stage.

Jeremy was super excited, not just because of the lineup, but because—in his mind—it was now officially a date.

There are no bad seats at the Opry, but the ones she selected were terrific—just to the left of center, lower level, front row. While the stars put on memorable performances, it was more about what happened in their two seats that was unforgettable. Jeremy slipped his arm around Kaitlin while the emcee made jokes, announced birthdays, and acknowledged the names of groups attending the show. She responded by snuggling and holding his other hand.

No doubt. Best day ever. Separately, yet together, they both watched their fingers intertwine. She teased him by lightly scratching his forearms with her long nails. He returned the favor by gently massaging her fingers. And they did this while pretending to listen to the music.

For Jeremy, it was as if history repeated itself. His parents had loved Country music, but tonight, he could care less about the music or really anything else. Every nerve in his body was attuned to this beautiful girl. Her hair was soft and silky. Her smile, captured on those lips he dreamed of so often, totally captivated him as the warmth of her body slowly drove him insane. He wanted her more than he'd ever wanted anyone... and that included Britany.

Damn it! Why did I have to think about her? Jeremy tried to force the thought of her out of his mind. With short blonde hair, the dark eye shadow a contrast to pale white skin, and her... *Damn you, Britany! Why couldn't you have been as beautiful inside as you were on the outside?* To nine hundred ninety-nine out of a thousand men, Britany would be judged prettier than Kaitlin. But

Jeremy knew in his heart Kaitlin was the true treasure in life.

When the show finally ended, Kaitlin turned to him. "Tell me truthfully. Did you like your surprise?"

His entire face beamed, "Absolutely perfect!" *Because you are here.* "Time for my surprise now. There are two places I want you to experience."

They sauntered to the gift shop, where he bought her a cute black tee-shirt with 'Grand Old Opry' across the front in sparkles. He also purchased her a keepsake, a print of that night's Opry lineup to remember their first date. At least in his mind it was a first date. They walked arm in arm across the parking lot to the old Opryland Hotel where they shared a banana split while strolling through the indoor gardens.

Walking back to the Suburban, they gazed at a sky filled with millions of stars. Pointing to the brightest one in the sky, he told her, "As a young man, I learned to look for the North Star, leaning on it to guide me. Let's make it our star, okay?"

She stopped, holding both his hands while searching his face. "You're thinking our friendship could turn out to be something quite special, aren't you?"

Yes, yes I do! Don't you?

The smile on her face was from ear to ear. When he nodded, she hugged him so tightly he thought she would break his ribs. She whispered, "I am beginning to think so, too."

They drove back to the Bed and Breakfast, taking a few moments to snuggle on the swing while reminiscing about the day. Jeremy didn't want the evening to end, but he heard her yawn.

"Getting late. May I walk you up to your room?"

"I would love that."

Unlocking the door for her, he checked to make sure it was safe. *Should I kiss her? Too soon?* She still stood in the hallway. Walking out, he reached for her hands.

Before he could react, she stood on tiptoes and lightly kissed his cheek. "Thank you for a wonderful day. I'm so glad we decided to be friends. I can't wait to see you in the morning. Good night."

He kissed her brow before crossing the hallway to his room. His heart was already missing her before he closed the door. His cell vibrated in his pocket. "Hello?"

"Hi. I wanted to make sure you made it safely to your room. I know it was a long and arduous journey." She giggled before continuing, "Would you mind if we talked for a few more minutes?"

He smiled, though she couldn't see it. "Sure! Anything in particular you want to talk about?"

"Actually, there is. I want to tell you about my favorite things and hear all about yours." When they finally finished, Jeremy happily dreamed about what lay in store for the morning.

Chapter 10

*K*aitlin woke up at four forty-five so she could be downstairs when Jeremy rose. She knew his habits, so she waited for him to come down for a run. He didn't disappoint. At precisely 5:00 A.M., she heard his footfalls on the stairs. *You're in for a surprise today, Mr. Roberts!*

She stood waiting in the darkness of the hallway and then whispered, "Morning, friend! Would you like some company on your run?"

His look of surprise was slowly replaced with joy. "What better way to start my day?" He was in much better shape than she was, and Kaitlin soon tired, but tried to keep the conversation lively. Even though the jog was almost an hour in length, it felt as if it were only a few minutes. Yesterday had been a blur, but a very enjoyable one. Her heart was trying to express things her mind didn't want to consider, yet.

After showers and a leisurely breakfast, they set out to explore Nashville. Kaitlin didn't like Country music—well, she didn't used to—but her tastes were rapidly changing. They spent the morning walking and talking, often holding hands.

For lunch, they decided to stop at an upscale bar on Music Row. As soon as they walked in, a short red-headed fellow let out a loud squeal and jumped over the bar, yelling, "Yee haw! Well if it ain't the L.T." He ran up to Jeremy and embraced him, pounding Jeremy's back with his fist. Jeremy did the same in return.

Turning to her, Jeremy introduced, "Ms. Kaitlin Jenkins, I am pleased to introduce you to Geeter Beauregard Smith, the original Nashville redneck."

Geeter removed his ball cap, bowing to Kaitlin. "Ma'am, it sure is a pleasure to meet y'all. I am at your service. Would y'all like to sit at a table or the bar?"

Kaitlin extended her hand, "Geeter, it's my pleasure to make your acquaintance. The bar is fine with me. So, why do you call Jeremy 'L.T.'?"

"That's 'cause he was my lieutenant back in the old Army days. Ma'am, I could tell you stories about him that would curl your toes!"

Really? Tell me, please! She smiled slyly, giving Jeremy a sidelong look. "Oh, he seems to have left some things out."

Jeremy said, "Now Kaitlin, you might not want to believe everything Geeter says because, well you know, the Iraqis got to him a little." He touched his forefinger to his temple before making the universal sign for crazy.

Geeter dug in his pockets as if looking for something, hooting, "Yeah, well, I got me papers from one of them Army docs sayin' I's sane, do you? I keep mine with me all the time in case anyone asks for 'em!" The good natured ribbing went on for several minutes until Jeremy asked where the restrooms were located. Geeter pointed to the steps leading one level down.

As Jeremy walked off, Geeter's accent became less redneck. He turned to face Kaitlin and said, "He's a great guy, ya know?"

She smiled. *I'm finding that out.*

Geeter's expression turned serious. "I wouldn't be alive today if it weren't for him. He saved my life in that hell hole."

Saved your life? Kaitlin looked at him curiously. "Are you being serious or are you exaggerating?"

Looking hurt, he said, "Ma'am, I may tell some tall tales, but L.T. is a true American hero. We were based outside of Baghdad. There were eighteen of us and we were doing recon in a force of four Humvees when we were ambushed."

Kaitlin gasped. "What?"

He nodded. "They hit the leading and trailing trucks with RPGs, stopping the column. We were trapped in a brutal cross fire. L.T. was in the third vehicle; I was in the second. Did I mention it was in the middle of a sand storm? They hit my Humvee, filling it with smoke. My driver and gunner crawled out. They took fire, both going down. I jumped out to drag them back inside to safety. Before I could, I took a couple of rounds in the back, but my armor saved me. Should have seen the bruises I had from that. When they hit me, I went down, striking my head on the frame. I blacked out for a few seconds."

He stopped to refill a drink for another patron, then returned to lean on the bar across from her.

"As I started to come to, I noticed that the sound of firing had been replaced by the howling wind of the storm. I opened my eyes, seeing figures running toward our unit, weapons at the ready. They were going to execute us. I rolled over, taking a bead on them. I tried to open fire, but the sand had jammed the action on my weapon. I was screwed. I knew I was going to die. I could hear their taunts as the closest one took aim not five foot away from me. Suddenly, L.T. comes rushing up from behind, laying down heavy fire. He charged into them without fear. I watched as he rolled up their position. His rush broke their attack. Then he organized us so we could fall back."

Geeter again stopped to fill a drink order for a waitress.

"After we got back to the fire base, he pulled us together for another attack, calling in choppers and fighter jets. If he hadn't attacked them when my weapon jammed, I wouldn't be here today. I owe my life to Lieutenant Roberts."

Oh my God! Kaitlin's eyes were open wide. "He never mentioned a word of that to me. Was he always like that?"

"Well, L.T. never had no fear, ever, but he was especially fearless that day. Of course, that was after he lost his aunt... and that bitch of a wife stabbed him in the back. He was the best man I ever served under. Biggest bad-ass in a unit of bad-asses."

Her face paled. *Jeremy has a wife? Would've been nice to know.* Then the words Geeter said came to her mind. *His wife stabbed him? Was that where the scars on his back came from?* Her curiosity got the better of her. "You said something about Jeremy getting stabbed in the back. What happened?"

"What? You didn't know? He got called to sick bay one day. Doc told him to strip so he could get his manhood examined. Seems his wife came down with syphilis. He didn't have it. Guess he wasn't one of her current sexual partners—get it?"

She did what? "What did Jeremy say?"

"Well, that wasn't what he signed up for when he married her. Damn, she tore his heart out, tramped it into the ground and then pissed on it. I wish I could have fragged her myself. You must be real special; I thought he swore off women forever."

Chapter 11

Jeremy softly approached Kaitlin, who appeared to be lost in thought. Softly jabbing her in the ribs, he asked, "Hey friend, did you miss me?"

For a moment, she simply glared at him. The look on her face was one he remembered well, the same expression she had given him for weeks when they first met.

He took a step backwards, looking into her eyes. What had happened while he was gone?

Suddenly, she jumped up, grabbing his hand firmly as her countenance turned to concern. She didn't let go for quite a while. He smiled, "Wow, if this is how you greet me, I should go to the bathroom more often." She slowly let go of her grip. He watched the changing of expression on her face. Concern filled his eyes as a look of anger filtered in. "Hey, are you okay? What's wrong? Did something happen?"

Her gaze locked on his for what seemed to be hours. She broke her trance by shaking her head, looking down. She took a deep breath before re-engaging him. "A funny thing happened while you were gone. Geeter told me about your wife. Imagine my surprise—a wife! I didn't know you were married. Kind of important, don't you think?"

He recoiled, "What exactly did he tell you?"

She hissed, "Everything. He told me everything."

For the first time, real anger flickered in his eyes. Then as swiftly as it came, it left. "Yeah, well, my big hearted and big mouthed redneck buddy never did know when to keep his mouth shut!"

All of her restraint flew out the window. "Keep his mouth shut? You weren't even going to tell me, were you? You lied to me."

His face sobered. "I didn't lie to you. I just didn't have the chance to tell you, yet. Yesterday was a day of happiness; I didn't want her name or her memories ruining it for me."

"What the... You're just angry because Geeter told me, because he gave away your dirty little secret. Didn't want me to know, did you? Things were just getting pretty cozy for you, weren't they? You never planned on telling me, admit it." Her voice was getting loud. People were starting to stare. "What else haven't you told me?"

Jeremy's face was turning red from embarrassment. He felt like punching Geeter for telling her about Britany. "I'm only angry at Geeter because it wasn't his story to tell."

Kaitlin screamed, apparently not caring that half of Nashville could hear her rants. "Damn you! Just when I started to trust you!"

"I wanted to tell you and would have, in time."

"Bullshit! That is unacceptable! How could you ever think that not telling me that you're... that you're..." She shoved her stool back, knocking it to the floor. Walking to the end of the bar, she used her hands to wipe her cheeks.

Geeter returned from the lower level, carrying a case of beer. He eyed Jeremy, asking, "Everything okay, L.T.?"

Had Jeremy been able to reach him, he would have broken his neck. "No," he muttered as he walked to

Kaitlin. *Dumb loud-mouthed redneck.* Jeremy walked so he stood behind Kaitlin. "Can we talk?"

She didn't bother looking at him. "No. I made a mistake opening up to you before. I thought you were different than other men, but you're no better."

"Can I please explain what really happened?"

Turning to shove her finger in his face, Kaitlin snarled, "I don't want to hear anything you have to say. I'm sorry I got involved with you. Sorry I offered friendship. Sorry I was stupid enough to trust you."

"Please give me a chance to explain. I don't want to lose your friendship."

She screamed, getting the attention of everyone in the bar. "You should have thought about that before you lied to me, you, you..."

What? "Like I said, I have never once lied to you."

"No? Why didn't you tell me you were married?"

He lowered his voice, hoping she would get the hint. "I didn't lie to you. I just didn't get a chance to tell you yet. I promised..."

"Promises? I know exactly what your promises mean... *nothing!*"

He stared at her, not understanding. "Okay, since you don't want to hear me out, what exactly do you want me to do?"

She shook her head as she glared at him. "Take me back to the Bed and Breakfast. I have had about all of Nashville, and you, that I can stand."

Didn't take long to screw this up. Jeremy nodded as he turned to get the check from Geeter.

When they pulled up in front of the large colonial house, he touched her hand before she could exit.

She hissed, "Get your hand off of me before I punch you!"

"I'm having a hard time understanding what just happened. We were so close, then..." His voice drifted off.

Kaitlin whipped around to face him. "Let's replay this, just so you can understand it. You were trying to position yourself to get me into bed, remember?"

Get you into bed? "I never once made a move on you or tried to do anything to..."

She slammed her hand against the dash. "You are such a liar! I can't believe you tried to get me to commit adultery with you!"

Adultery? He was almost sick to his stomach. He whispered, "I'm sorry. I didn't know you were married."

Her face turned blood red as she screamed at him. "I'm not the one who's married. You are! Geeter told me."

He slowly removed his hand from hers. "So Geeter told you I was married and you believed him. Right away you jump to the conclusion I only want to sleep with you. I didn't think you were the type of person who judged other people. Guess I was the fool, wasn't I?"

Her eyes narrowed as she stared at him curiously. "What are you talking about?"

Jeremy backed away from her. "Geeter told you I was married, didn't he?"

She nodded.

"Did he tell you I had a wife?"

"Y-y-yes."

"Did he also tell you I divorced her, oh say, about eight years ago? I don't have a wife, I have an *ex*-wife."

Chapter 12

Kaitlin stared at the man sitting across the table from her. His head was down; he had yet to look at her face. It was Monday afternoon. Jeremy had finished giving her his daily update. "Anything else you want me to include in the report?"

"No. In my opinion, this town is as evil as the last one."

She couldn't focus on work. She didn't know what to do next. She had apologized for the misunderstanding and he told her not to worry—it didn't matter. But since then, he'd been so distant. She was very attracted to him, but in her mind, he had lied. Okay, he didn't actually lie, but the omission felt like a lie. It scared her that his eyes had been vacant ever since he told her he was divorced. She wished things would go back to how they had been, but she didn't have a clue how to get there.

Her brows were furrowed as she watched him. "So now what? Are you suggesting we dump this town, too?"

"That's up to you. You're the boss."

At least look at me, Jeremy. A few days ago, he had called her his friend, not his boss. *Then I told you I regretted befriending you.* Saddened, she shook her head. "We'll finish the rest of the evaluation tomorrow."

He looked away. "I have a bad feeling about this town. I would advise you to stay in the motel, not for me, but for you."

I need to think this through. It's not fair to either of us to go on like this.

Absentmindedly nodding, she replied quietly, "I'll take that under advisement. Good night."

He frowned, quickly standing to leave. "Okay. Night, Kaitlin."

She watched him shuffle toward the elevator, head down. The situation was wearing on him, too. Maybe she should just throw in the towel and go home. She wanted a deeper relationship with him, but she didn't have a clue if he even wanted that anymore. He seemed to have completely shut down on her. She needed to do some soul searching. If there was any hope to get past this, she should continue on the trip. If not, she needed to ask John Stange to find a replacement for her. The attraction between them was deep, but dangerous.

She wiped an errant strand of hair from her face. A deeper relationship meant allowing him completely into her heart. Doing so would make her vulnerable. Her concern came from her past. Caring about Jeremy wasn't even a question; she did, very much. *The real question is: can we get past this?* That was what she needed to decide. Before she closed her eyes tonight, she would make a choice one way or another.

With a monumental burden on her shoulders, she took a walk. Her mind was completely lost in thought as she walked along aimlessly. She finally sat for a long time in a park on an old splintered bench. What would life be like with him or, worse yet, without him?

Why did everything have to be so hard? She wasn't the only one with issues; Jeremy had problems he had suffered through, too. *Why couldn't I have been the first woman you fell for?* It would have been so much easier if he hadn't been married before, or if he simply would have told her about it before she found out from someone else. *Before I misunderstood Geeter's story and unloaded on you.*

Kaitlin watched the sun start to set. Suddenly, it became crystal clear. Her heart happily won the battle as she finally made up her mind. She formulated a plan.

She whispered out loud, "I need to talk to you, tonight. As soon as I get back to the motel, you and I will talk and someway, somehow, we will get past this. We need to, for both our sakes."

As she stood to go, a loud voice brought her back to the present. *What the...* Blinking her eyes to get out of her thoughts, she heard it again. It wasn't one voice, it was three. Three haggard looking white men in their early twenties were close by, talking loudly. They were staring at her. Their speech was vulgar. Kaitlin's skin tingled in disgust as she realized they were talking about her! They were making nasty comments about the way she looked and what they wanted to do to her. Their repulsive words felt like rats climbing up her spine.

Surveying her surroundings, she realized she didn't have a clue where she was. Her head had been so lost in thought that she hadn't been paying attention. It was almost dark. No one else was in sight. *I've got to get out of here!*

She was in a lonely section of a park. A street ran alongside it, separated by a fence, but there was no traffic on the road.

Quickly, she stood, walking away from the three men. Stealing a quick peek behind her, she saw the three men following, calling after her with the most horrible things she had ever heard. The filth they spewed forth turned her stomach. When two of them started running along the fence to her right, it dawned on her that they were hoping to block her from the gate that would allow her to get to the street and freedom.

She turned to see the biggest one closing in on her. He shouted, "Hey you! Wait up. Let's get to know each other a little." She turned away.

He yelled, "Don't walk away when I call you. Hey, I'm talking to you! Git back here. You got something we want."

The other men weren't at the gate yet. Maybe she could make it to the street before they got there.

She sprinted forward faster than ever, fueled by her fight or flight reflex, but they beat her to the opening by twenty feet. The two smaller men turned, slowly walking toward her as they herded her away from the street. She ignored the sharp muscle cramp yanking at her leg. They leered at her, making filthy comments about what they were going to make her do to them. She turned to find the big man only ten feet away. With one more glance at the deserted street, she emblazoned the street names in her mind.

If I keep running, I'll have to go deeper into the park. God, help me. I'm in trouble, serious trouble.

"Help! Help!" she screamed as she started to sprint away. "Somebody help me!"

Quick! Call 911.

She pulled her cell from her pocket, but before she could dial, Jeremy's number lit up her phone.

She punched the button, and heard him yell, "Where are you?"

The men were closing in on her. "I need help! I'm in a park off of Spring and Lombard. Three men are chasing me and..." Her scalp screamed out in pain as one of them grabbed her by the hair, using his leverage to throw her to the ground. His weight on top of her knocked her breath from her body. With horror, she pleaded, "Help, Jeremy! There are three men..."

The pain in her wrist as he clamped his hand around it was intense. He yanked the cell from her, and laughed into it. "She can't come to the phone right now. She's too busy having fun!" He threw the device aside. By now the other two men reached her. Her face stung as she was slapped. Pain radiated in her arms and stomach as they pinched unmercifully.

This can't be happening! "Help. Somebody help me!"

Before she could say anything else, the air was forced from her lungs as the fat one pounced on her chest with his knees. Painfully, her arms were slammed to the ground by the other two, pinning her with her back to the earth. The feeling of helplessness pervaded as the fat one roughly wrapped his hands around her throat. She couldn't get her breath. Everything started to fade to darkness until the left side of her face and cheekbone stung from his slap. *God, please help me!*

She gulped the air and coughed violently. The big one was still on top of her. He spoke quickly, lust in his eyes. "Here's the deal. You belong to us, now. Don't struggle and you don't get hurt. We're gonna move this little party somewhere more private. Scream out and I'll strangle you again. Fight back and I'll cut you! I'll skin you alive, understand?"

Her airway momentarily clear, Kaitlin screamed once more, "Help! Somebody please..." True to his word, the man wrapped his hands around her throat, but this time with even more violence and pressure. Her body convulsed as the intense pressure wracked through her. She had to fight the urge to throw up.

His laughing face was the last thing Kaitlin saw before she blacked out.

A sudden pain in her stomach brought her back to consciousness. She could no longer fight off the nausea. She tried to move her head, but couldn't, so the vomit choked her. They had her restrained by her head. She struggled, but her hands and feet were also tied tightly, spread eagled, stretched out but standing against a chain link fence. Her voice was hoarse as she squealed, "Please help me! Somebody, please help!" She couldn't move. Her body trembled uncontrollably as tears of fear started to fill her eyes.

The big one laughed as he stood in front of her. His lips felt like a dirty piece of leather as he started to kiss her face, running his tongue down her neck. She couldn't move, so she spit in his face. "Get off of me, you bastard!" Sudden pain reported in from her eye as she saw his fist make contact.

Happy place! Find a happy place. She forced her mind to see the beach at Maui, where she and her sister Kelly frolicked in the waves. She remembered her older siblings, Cassie and Tina, holding her on their laps as they read stories to her as a child. She suddenly remembered Jeremy and the joy of their conversation in the car.

A cold feeling came to her neck. Coming back to the present, she saw the fat one holding a knife against her throat. He smiled evilly as he forced the stiff, menacing object tighter against her skin.

She pleaded, "No, please no!"

He was breathing rapidly. "I don't think you appreciate your situation."

Happy place. She was shopping and laughing with her mom. She was walking down a lane, holding her father's hand as he told her he had raised four princesses, but she was his favorite.

Her body rattled as he shook her. "Pay attention to me! Let's try this again. You will do exactly what I say, and you'll do it when I tell you." The coldness of the blade pierced her thoughts. "Understand?" When she didn't answer right away, he increased the pressure. "Answer me. What're you gonna let me do?"

This will not be the defining moment of my life. I will survive and find happiness again. The pain increased as he drove it harder against her skin. She whimpered, "Anything."

He's too fat to do anything to me here.

"You'll do whatever I want or I'll gut you like a pig. You belong to me and I control you, understand?"

She spit in his face. "Never! You will never control me. Do *you* understand?"

He laughed as he wiped her spittle from his face. "We'll just see about that." Kaitlin fought back the sensation to again throw up as the flat of his knife traced her legs, across her stomach, her chest, and stopped at her throat. "Put up a struggle, bitch, and I'll do it. I'll cut your throat! Dead or alive, I'll take what I want from you."

God, please don't let them hurt me! The lustful look in the big man's eyes told her that he hoped she'd fight back. He might just kill her for the fun of it whether she struggled or not.

Kaitlin wanted to break free, but they had her tied fast. Her attackers knew she was helpless, completely at their whims. She didn't have a prayer.

I will not go down without a fight. I will forget you, but if I get the opportunity, I can guarantee you will never forget me.

The fat one slowly unbuckled his belt and the top of his pants. Smiling, he told the other two, "Help the lady out of her things and get her on the ground."

Her skin recoiled as she felt one of their tongues across her face, while another grabbed her blouse, smiling as he ripped it partially open. Then many things happened in quick succession.

Her heartbeat was pounding so loudly that at first she was barely aware of the sounds or the lights. A horn blew repeatedly and the loud scream of a powerful engine filled the air. The high beams of a speeding, dark SUV bounced across the park's shaggy lawn, its wheels catching air before lighting down on the basketball court.

"Help!" Kaitlin screamed with renewed hope. "Someone please help me!"

The squeal of braking tires on the macadam rent the damp night air. As if in a dream, Jeremy jumped out of the big black vehicle, not saying a word. Catching only a glimpse in the dim light, his expression scared even her.

The fat man pointed at Jeremy and told the two smaller men, "Get rid of that asshole." Jeremy turned to meet them as he flung his coat onto the hood of the Suburban. He purposefully approached.

The two men charged. The one to Kaitlin's right reached him first. Jeremy pivoted off his right foot, drilling the first one with a vicious punch to the solar plexus. Kaitlin winced at the sickening sound of breaking ribs, then watched her assailant drop to his knees. Two more violent blows rained down on the unmoving pile of flesh.

Jeremy turned to meet the second threat. The man pulled a knife and rushed forward. Deftly stepping aside, Jeremy grabbed the man's wrist and slammed his knee against the man's forearm. Even at a distance, she could hear more bones break.

The man screamed as his arm flopped uselessly. Jeremy delivered a roundhouse kick with such force that she could see teeth fly out of her assailant's mouth, bouncing like marbles on the basketball court in the lights of the SUV. The second man ceased moving.

Jeremy picked up the knife and headed for the last attacker. Kaitlin felt the man's sweaty hands on her cheek as the sharpness of his knife again pushed against her throat.

"Drop it!" yelled the fat man, staring at the blade in Jeremy's hand. "Take one more step and I'll cut her throat!"

I don't want to die! Please, don't let him kill me!

Jeremy stopped, gripping the blade he held with both hands. In awe, Kaitlin watched him snap it in two as if it were a matchstick, throwing it to the ground.

The pressure against her throat lessened as her assailant's mouth dropped. He nervously snickered, "Get the hell out of here before I cut you to shreds!"

Kaitlin saw Jeremy's eyes scan the scene.

Her attacker cursed at him again, holding the knife up for Jeremy to see.

With the quickness of a jaguar pouncing on its prey, Jeremy sprang forward, rushing his opponent. He charged, straight arming the fat man in the chest.

The assailant tried to defend himself by sweeping the knife in a quick arc, which sliced into Jeremy's arm.

Kaitlin yelped in fear when she saw blood coursing down Jeremy's arm. Without hesitation, Jeremy grabbed the other man's shirt, pivoted and continued to follow through, throwing the obese man roughly to the ground. Jeremy now stood between Kaitlin and her attacker.

The man with the knife crawled to his feet and rushed back at Jeremy. In amazement, Kaitlin watched as Jeremy slammed both his hands against the extended arm of the assailant, easily plucking the knife from his grasp. The man looked on in astonishment, first at his empty hand then at the knife Jeremy was now holding.

Jeremy didn't flinch, as unruffled in combat as he'd been in his daily reports.

The big man took a step back, holding his hands in the air, "Whoa, it was just a big misunderstanding, man. Let's talk about this."

Jeremy dropped the knife on the ground at Kaitlin's feet as he took confident and calculated strides forward.

The big guy turned to run, but the ex-Ranger was quicker. Jeremy grabbed him by the hair, then dropped him with a quick kick to the knees while violently twisting his right arm behind his back.

"Aaaaah, stop! You're hurting me!" the big man screamed.

Kaitlin winced at the loud popping noise which pulled the shoulder out of joint. The man screamed in pain.

Jeremy's hand grasped the screaming man's face. "Shut your mouth, now or I will really hurt you, are we clear on that?"

The man bit his lips as he crawled away, looking like a three-legged crab.

Jeremy retrieved the knife and turned toward Kaitlin, anger still evident in his eyes. He brought the blade up to the side of her face.

"Oh my God, *no!* Jeremy, *don't hurt me!*" Kaitlin screamed.

His expression changed to emptiness as he stared at her, knife suspended adjacent to her eyes. Jeremy shook his head as his expression turned to sadness. He flicked the knife and shred the rope which was binding Kaitlin's left wrist beside her head, then followed with the opposite side.

Kaitlin's body collapsed, half in fear and half relief, as Jeremy caught her weight against his shoulder. Shifting her slightly to reposition her torn blouse, he then swiftly dealt with the rope at her feet.

"I think I'm going to throw up," she mumbled.

With strong but gentle arms, he carried her to the Suburban, whispering softly, "You're safe now."

The leather seat felt cool against her skin.

Jeremy tried to examine her wounds. "Where does it hurt the worst?"

"My eye," she answered, squinting on the left.

He gently touched all around the socket. "I don't think anything's broken, but we should get you to the ER just to make sure."

"N-n-no!" Kaitlin protested. "Can we just leave now, please?"

"You sure?"

"Yes, but wait. He cut you. How bad is it?"

"It's only a flesh wound."

"But Jeremy..."

His eyes sought hers as he briefly touched her hand. "I only care about you. We'll head back to the motel if that's what you want."

"Please?"

Jeremy looked doubtful, but gently turned her body, tucking and buckling her into the seat. He retrieved his jacket from the hood, then wrapped it around her. Finally he reclaimed Kaitlin's purse from the lot and set it on the seat between them.

They had only driven two blocks when Kaitlin said, "Pull over!"

Jeremy swerved to the shoulder of the road and reached across her to pop open her door. As she tipped to the right, retching, he lightly swept her hair back.

Another bout of nausea struck, but she fought it off. Jeremy pulled her back in.

"How're you feeling?"

"I don't know how I can make it to my room."

"Don't worry. Got that covered," he said.

"What?"

"Just trust me, okay?"

Kaitlin didn't answer out loud. *I do, completely.*

Chapter 13

*J*eremy drove the Suburban to a drug store. If Kaitlin didn't want to go to a hospital, he would have to care for her wounds. His examination didn't reveal anything overly serious, but he knew she was in pain. Of more concern to him was the fear she might go into shock, which would be more dangerous than her injuries.

Jeremy turned to face her, "I need to go inside and get a couple supplies. You can stay here if you like."

Kaitlin shivered as her eyes engaged his.

He added, "You'll be safe; that I promise you, on my life."

Slowly she replied, "I don't think I can walk that far."

"Okay, lock the door and we'll talk on the phone the whole time. If you get scared, tell me and I'll be out here in less than ten seconds, okay?"

"Promise?"

"I promise. Here, you'll need this." He handed her iPhone back before putting on a long-sleeved shirt to cover his bleeding arm.

Jeremy climbed out and circled around to her side of the Suburban, placing the call to Kaitlin's cell. She picked up and he said, "Okay, let's do this. I want you to keep a close watch, especially on your six."

She gave him a strange look through the glass. "My six? What are you talking about?"

"Oh, that's right, you're a civilian. So here is what you do." Jeremy pointed as he spoke. "Pretend you're in the center of a big clock, with the number twelve in front of you. Behind you is your six. To your right is your three and to your left is your nine, got it?"

"Okay, I remember Gibbs explaining this on NCIS."

"I guess TV does have a purpose," he laughed. "May I ask a personal question?"

"S-s-sure," she answered hesitantly.

"Are you dyslexic?"

"No, but why does that matter?"

"Because if you were, your nine would be your three and your three your nine." He smiled, but she gave him a skeptical look. He knew he needed to do something to keep her mind off the trauma she had been through. He turned to enter the store. "Now if you need me, we should come up with some elaborate code word. If you say this word, then I'll drop everything and come running. Do you have any ideas?" *Just stay with me, honey.*

"Jeremy..." she sighed.

"Nope, you might actually say my name by accident. Try again."

"I don't know."

"Too complex. Try again!" He could hear her impatient huff, and it made him almost smile.

"How about 'help'?"

"That's better."

He stood next to a display of candy, watching her sitting in the vehicle outside. The young male clerk eyed him with suspicion, staring at the growing red stain on his shirt sleeve. He returned the clerk's glare. *Yeah, you think I'm weird. But I don't really care.*

"I'm good. Can you just get finished so we can go?"

"Yes, but I'll be there if you call. Agreed?"

He saw her nod through the window and he turned to go down the first aisle.

"Well, I see you just nodded your head, but your smartphone is too dumb to tell me that. You'll need to enunciate, just a little, okay?"

She sighed loudly, "Whatever! Yes, that's fine."

Ibuprofen to reduce the swelling. "How's your six?"

"Fine."

Extra strength Acetaminophen for the pain. "How about your nine?"

"Also fine."

Triple antibiotic ointment to prevent infection. "How about your four twenty-three?"

That got a little snort from her. "Mine is fine, how's yours?"

He smiled. "Oh, it's doing quite well, but I didn't know you cared. I've been doing a little exercise regime to work on that particular part of my body."

"Don't get too excited."

Hydrogen peroxide and cotton balls to clean the wounds. "How can I not get excited? I'm talking with my boss, who by the way is my favorite person of all time. Yes, ma'am. Oh look, they're running a special in here. Buy eleven rolls of toilet paper and get the twelfth one free, however, there is one stipulation."

"What's that?"

"How's your seven?"

"Stop it! Just get done!"

He repeated, "How is your seven?"

Another sigh, "A little sore, but surviving. Now, what was the toilet paper stipulation?"

"You have to buy the toilet paper in a twelve-pack, get it?"

"Yep, got it. Are you gonna buy the twelve-pack?" she asked.

"You want me to buy a twelve-pack of toilet paper?"

"No, you idiot! I was only acknowledging your ridiculous sense of humor."

"So, no toilet paper, huh? That's kind of gross." He picked out a tube of topical pain reliever.

There was a brief pause, "I think there is something wrong with you, Jeremy."

"My doctor has been saying that for years, but guess what?"

"What?"

"This is the longest non-work conversation we've had in a while."

Again, she sighed loudly. "Is that a fact?"

"Yes, but there is a problem."

"Now what?"

"This is a crappy conversation. Know why?"

She again sighed loudly, "No, why?"

"Because we're talking about poop."

"You're the one who brought up toilet paper. And it's disturbing how you were deeply intrigued with that subject. Nice try. Didn't I tell you I minored in psychology?"

"Yeah, why?"

"Oh, I was thinking since you're so interested in poop that Freud might say you are regressing to the anal stage of psycho-sexual development. Just saying, you know?"

"Cute," he said.

"Thanks, I'll take that as a compliment."

He changed his voice to a deep Southern drawl. "Did I ever tell you about the time Geeter and I were driving around drinking beer in his hot rod Dodge Challenger R/T?"

"I didn't know you drank," she said.

Need something with protein and sugar. "Only to be sociable," he responded, picking up her favorite coconut macaroons. "So anyway, me and Geeter were driving around and there's like forty empty beer bottles in the back seat and lo and behold, these blue lights start flashing behind us."

"Oh no, the police?" She sounded concerned.

He smiled. *Really into this, aren't you? Good!* "So I looked over at Geeter and he drawls, 'Don't worry about it, son. I got this.' So he peels off a label from one of the bottles, sticks it on his forehead, and puts his hat back on. This cop comes up, shines a bright light in the car and asks, 'You boys been drinkin?' Geeter says, 'Yes sir, but it's all right.' He then pulled off his hat and says, 'See! I's on the patch'!" Jeremy made it to the checkout, stuck behind an old lady with about ninety items in her cart.

Kaitlin was silent for a moment. "That story wasn't true, was it?"

Of course not, but it occupied your mind, didn't it? He dropped the redneck accent. "No, not at all."

"Are you coming out soon?"

"As soon as I pay the bill." He heard her sigh. "Why don't we play a game?"

"A game? What game?"

"I'll take that as a yes. Now, I want you to close your eyes," he said, then revised, "but keep one on your six. So close your left eye and pretend it's covering for both of your eyes, okay?"

"Jeremy, you're certifiably nuts. I don't have the time or patience for this. There's definitely something very seriously wrong with you, do you know that?"

"My psychologist says the same thing every time I talk to him. Now here's what I want you to do. I want you to concentrate on one word, ready?"

Again, a moment of hesitation, "Go ahead," she sighed, "but do you really see a psychologist?"

I probably should, but no. "Absolutely! On the third Thursday of the sixth week each month. Now, I want you to think of elephants, you know with the big floppy ears, hairy tails, tusks, and those adorable trunks? Think only of them, then tell me when all you are thinking about are elephants, okay?"

Once again, she sighed loudly, "Like I have a choice. Okay, I'm thinking of elephants."

"Only elephants?"

"Yes."

"You're not thinking of foxes, are you?"

She screamed into the phone, "No, Jeremy! I am only thinking of elephants."

"Or penguins?"

"Damn you! No, I am not thinking of penguins, only elephants!"

"Great. Now comes the fun part, ready?"

"Sure."

It looks like my plan was a success! He signed the credit card bill. "Now, I don't want you to think about elephants. So, please tell me. What are you thinking about now?"

She snorted. "I am thinking about how much I hate you right now... except that I just realized you've been distracting me so I wouldn't be worried."

Jeremy walked out and waved to her, then opened the door, asking, "Did it work?"

She nodded her tired head. "Yes, perfectly. Thank you." Her pretty lips start to curl into a grin.

Chapter 14

Kaitlin was still fighting back nausea when they arrived at their motel. Actually, her foggy mind was quite impressed with Jeremy's little conversation to distract her at the pharmacy. She knew he had tried to get her to laugh, but she wasn't sure she would ever laugh again.

He opened her car door and gently picked her up in strong arms, carrying her to the room.

Her whole body trembled as she stared into his blue eyes.

Jeremy smiled at her sadly. "It's okay. You'll soon be locked safely in your room."

Kaitlin quickly shook her head. "I don't think I can manage by myself. Would you... stay with me?" she asked in a meek whisper. "I'd feel much safer if you were here."

"You will be safe, I promise." He unlocked the room door and placed her on top the bedspread. The softness of the mattress was comforting. Even though Jeremy had arrived in time to save her life—and her honor—she still felt violated.

While she struggled to find feelings of normalcy, Jeremy glanced at her face as he started cleaning the scrapes with hydrogen peroxide. His words surprised and concerned her. "I'm sorry. I'm to blame. I should have been there for you."

"This wasn't your fault." She shook her head, but immediately regretted it. The dizziness returned with a vengeance. As Jeremy used a cotton ball to apply antibiotic ointment to the scratches on her neck, she remembered his knife wound. "Your arm! We should get you to a doctor. Your shirt is soaked with blood."

"I'm fine. Nothing more than a scratch."

Like hell. Your arm is still bleeding.

"It's more than a scratch. You might need stitches."

He nodded his head as he rubbed something around her eye that brought tears, but provided immediate relief from her pain. "Okay. I'll go if you do." He laughed a little when he saw her smirk. "I'm fine. Don't worry about me."

Her skin felt like she had insects crawling on her. "I really want to get out of these dirty clothes," she said. She felt so hopeless and helpless because she didn't even have the energy to change her own clothes.

Jeremy stopped, his eyes searching her face in disbelief. "Okay," he said, before adding hesitantly, "How would you like me to help you?"

They discussed it, and Jeremy gently removed Kaitlin's sneakers and socks. The room had two queen-sized beds. He stripped the top sheet off the second bed while she managed to unbuckle her belt, and open the top of her jeans. Then Jeremy covered her legs with the sheet. Once she understood what he was doing, she laid back and pulled the bed linen up while he pulled her jeans off from the bottom. Then raising her arms above her, Jeremy peeled off her shirt, closing his eyes, turning his head away.

She wrapped the loose sheet around her body, anxious to see if he would turn around. When he didn't, she finally said, "All set," then added a meek, "thank you."

He looked back and wrapped the blankets around her, tucking her in tightly. Jeremy folded her clothes and laid them on the dresser. Kaitlin was touched by not only his concern, but something else that was becoming quite obvious. She tucked that away for later.

Am I really seeing what I think I see in your eyes?

He helped prop her up so she could take the painkillers, advising her to chew the pills so the medication could get into her bloodstream quicker. Thoughtfully, he handed her a coconut macaroon to wash away the taste.

She nibbled in tiny bites, thinking Jeremy seemed to remember even the smallest of details. Macaroons were her favorite.

"How long until my headache goes away? My head hurts from them yanking my hair."

"It'll take a few minutes. Maybe this will help." He gently began to massage her scalp, easing the pain. His hands were so gentle. The same hands whose knuckles were bruised and bloody from coming to her rescue.

The tingling where his fingers touched contrasted with the rest of her body, which felt as if some vile animal had defecated on her. "I want a shower, but I don't think I can stand up."

"I can run a bath for you," Jeremy suggested, "if you think you can manage."

By the look on his face, she could tell he was struggling with something. She thought about it for a moment and answered, "A bath would be nice but I'm not sure how I could possibly manage that."

"If you trust me, I can help you. But after what you went through, I can easily see why you wouldn't want a man, especially me, to help you. In fact, if you want me to leave, I will, right now."

Panic filled her. "Oh no, please don't leave me!" She swallowed hard, "I mean, well, I don't want you to see me naked, but…" She blushed.

"I don't want to see you naked either," he said. "But I can carry you in and bring you towels."

You don't want to see me naked? She bit her lip before replying, "Okay, I really want to get cleaned off."

Jeremy turned on the water in the tub and gave Kaitlin another sheet to cover herself. He returned to gently pick her up. She noticed how strong he was, how gently he touched her back and knees to carry and place her cautiously in the warm bath.

"Call me when you're done," he said, and closed the door behind him.

Seeing the dark bruises already forming on her body, Kaitlin sobbed into the washcloth. Tonight had been humiliating.

When she finished all she could manage, she drained the water, drying herself as best as she could. The contrast between the beasts who had mauled her body and this tall man who now comforted her made her mind a little foggy. "Jeremy," she called. "Can you come help me?"

It was almost comical. First she saw his hands come through the door, carrying yet another sheet, this time outstretched like a timid bullfighter entering the ring.

At the edge of the tub, his hand accidentally touched her bare skin. "I'm sorry, I'm sorry," he said. "I'm so sorry! I didn't mean to touch you there!"

She shook her head. "You need to learn anatomy. That was my shoulder."

His relief was audible.

For the first time since the attack, Kaitlin actually smiled.

He gently wrapped and carried her back to the bed, drying her back with a towel then tucking her in under the sheets and blankets. "Is there a particular suitcase you want me to bring over?"

"Yes, the one with the Pan Am tag."

After placing it at the foot of the bed, he turned to give her privacy. "Call when you're done," he said as he carried the bag from the pharmacy to the bathroom.

It took her a while, but she managed to slip into some sweats. "Jeremy, you can come out now."

She noticed he had used the time in the bathroom to cover his wound while she was dressing. He quickly returned her suitcase to the floor.

"Well, it looks like you're good for the night," he said as he prepared to leave. "Anything else before I go?"

She grasped his hand tightly. *Don't you dare leave me!* Instead, she whispered, "I don't want to be alone tonight."

He smiled sadly and brushed a stray lock of hair from her eyes. "Okay. I won't go anywhere unless you tell me to leave."

Chapter 15

Jeremy found sleep impossible to come by with a bruised and battered Kaitlin tightly clinging to his arm. While Kaitlin slept a troubled sleep, he was concerned she would drift deeper into shock as the realization of the attack sunk in. He prayed she would have no long lasting impact from the assault.

Six times that night she had bolted awake; Jeremy was there, watchful each time. He made sure not to restrain her, but to be like a rock she could cling to. He waited until she crawled back to him, trembling as she wrapped herself tightly around his arm. Each time, he would murmur soft words of comfort until she stopped shaking.

Jeremy knew he had failed in his duty, the duty to protect her. This was all his fault. He was the reason she had been assaulted. It felt like he personally delivered each bruise, cut, and scrape. Civilian life wasn't like being in the service, where he could order her not to go out into what he considered an unsafe and dangerous environment. He hadn't anticipated her quick departure the previous evening. He thought she would go for a walk, but expected that she would wait a little while. He knew she was contemplating how she felt, whether she could really trust him. *Certainly screwed that up!*

Shaking his head at the ceiling, he thought how betrayed she must have felt. He had fully intended to tell her about Britany—but on his terms, not Geeter's. *I mean, you just don't go up to someone you really like and say, 'Hi, my slutty ex-wife destroyed my life, so I'm a little tender inside.'* Really, what else could he have done? He still didn't know.

He had blown his chance with Kaitlin. His experiment in civilian life had failed miserably. There was only one option left—to return to service. His ex-CO had called yesterday, asking him to return. The door was still open. The Rangers had one more mission for him, to lead the best soldiers in the world into war, one more deployment back into hell. After that, he could finish his doctorate in History and hopefully live out his career at West Point, teaching military history. That was the only thing left that he might possibly be good at. He sure wasn't good at love. If he had been, he and Britany might still be married. It was time to be a Ranger again.

His mind went back to the previous evening. He had already been out looking for her when he called. Thank God she had enough presence of mind to give him a location to start searching.

No, he couldn't go on trying to protect her when she didn't even want him doing it.

Suddenly, she bolted upright, again. He waited patiently as her fears subsided, until she settled against him. She needed help, love, and comfort. After what had happened between them, he knew he wasn't the one to provide those things. He had blown it. In the morning, he would convince her to return to her family, where she would be cared for, loved, and protected. While she was away, he would quietly resign and return to the service. She wouldn't ever have to face him again.

But as he held her, his vision became blurry. Everything he really wanted in life, he held in his arms right now. *Kaitlin*. Without saying as much, he had already confessed it. He loved her.

Even though her face was covered with bruises and cuts, she was still the most beautiful girl he had ever seen, so exquisite, so full of life. What would it have been like to share his life with her?

Perfect.

He wanted to know everything about this delicate woman, her memories, her fears, her hopes and dreams. What would it have been like to wake up to see her beautiful face each morning, to have her face be the last thing he saw at night?

Heaven.

He longed to watch the sunrise with her, to dance in the rain with her, to walk along the beach of life with her hand in his.

It will never be.

She stirred again in her sleep, softly murmuring for help. He kissed her forehead as he held her hand tightly. That seemed to quell the fears of her dreams. Again his mind wandered; what would it be like to lift her veil, to kiss her lips and promise his undying love to her and her alone, forever?

But that was only a pipe dream.

Roberts, you are one sorry-assed excuse for a man!

As he looked back over the last few days, he knew she had realized she made a mistake offering her friendship. But no one had ever tried to be his friend the way she had on his mother's birthday. Not even Britany. The door of opportunity had been right there. Eternal bliss was at his fingertips. *And you let it slip through your hands, you stupid bastard.*

This whole thing had been his fault. If he'd just told her he had been married before, they wouldn't have quarreled. If they hadn't quarreled, she wouldn't have taken that walk. If she hadn't taken that walk, the whole attack never would have happened. He was the cause of her pain.

Jeremy knew what he had to do. He would take today to help her calm down, to regain her composure, to steady herself. Tomorrow, he would get her home, and then he would leave.

Wiping his cheeks, he gently untangled his body from hers and put on his shoes. With his mind made up, it would be easier to get through this day without hurting her any more. After calling his CO, he would put on a happy face and bring her breakfast. He needed to come up with a plan on how to convince her to return to Chicago. That was what she needed. Chicago, a place of love with her family, her friends there to love her. Chicago, the place where he would wave goodbye and walk out of her life, forever.

Chapter 16

As Kaitlin opened her eyes, she had no idea why her mind was filled with fear. She and Jeremy had talked all night long, getting past their problems, hadn't they? But she wasn't holding him. She was holding a pillow.

Was it a dream? *If it was, I want to go back to sleep.* Suddenly, the beautiful dream was replaced by memories of the terrifying nightmare she had. Three men had attacked her! Then out of nowhere, Jeremy had rescued her.

Her head was pounding; her whole body was sore. She looked around the room, noticing she was all alone. *Was he really here or am I losing it?* If he had been there, why did he leave? She began to think she had dreamt the worst nightmare of her life, but her throat and face hurt. She pulled back the neck line of her sweatshirt, seeing the dark bruise on her stomach. *Oh my God, it wasn't a dream.*

Her head started to pound as her chest suddenly became tight, making it difficult to draw even the slightest breath. Standing unsteadily, she looked in the mirror, noting the bruises and cuts on her face and neck as well as a terrible black eye. *Oh God.* Her thoughts drifted and she recalled how gently Jeremy had cared for her. And she remembered asking him to stay.

She stood, looking around the room. "Are you in here?" There was no answer. She fought back terror. *What if they came back?* What if they were waiting outside for her? What if they had taken Jeremy?

Kaitlin's senses were on high alert. She heard the shuffling sound of footsteps approaching outside the door, and then loudly, the lock clicked open. Her chest tightened further as she surveyed the room like a cornered and desperate animal, grabbing the only weapon she could quickly find—a high-heeled shoe. Kneeling partially behind one of the beds, she cocked her arm and prepared to defend herself.

The door swung fully open as Jeremy backed into the room, carrying a tray laden with food and coffee. She tried to hide the evidence of her panic, but not in time.

Fighting back laughter, Jeremy placed the tray on the bed and raised his hands, stating in his best Southern accent, "I surrender, ma'am. Please, oh please, don't beat me with your shoe."

Her anger overflowed as she threw the high heel, hitting him squarely in the head. Tears blurred her vision. She turned away, placing a hand over her mouth.

Jeremy must have realized he had scared her. Smile gone, he was by her side, gently touching her shoulder. "Katie, I am sorry. I shouldn't have laughed at you."

Sobbing slightly, she said, "I may not have your Kung Fu skills, but I did my best." She turned quickly, jabbing his chest with her fore-finger and added, "And I quit being Katie in college. Never, ever, ever, call me Katie! Do you understand?"

"Yes, ma'am, I am sorry. Can you forgive me?"

She roughly shoved him out of the way so she could move to the mirror.

He followed her, his image appearing behind hers. "Are you all right?"

"Look at my face. I don't know if there is enough makeup in the world to cover this crap. Have you ever seen anything this ugly?"

Staring into her eyes through the looking glass, he replied softly, "I only see a beautiful woman who was attacked. Nothing will ever change that. Even if you lost your hair and became a leper, I would still think you looked beautiful."

She looked down at the floor to hide her blush. With pursed lips she said, "I am not beautiful. Not before... and definitely not now. Not ever."

"Oh, yes you are. I know you went through hell last evening. Want to talk?" She didn't respond, but instead stared blankly at the floor. A quiet and uneasy silence followed, broken by his next question, "Would you like something to eat? I brought coffee, bacon, fruit, eggs, and potatoes. And I even raided the half-and-half bin because I know you love them."

"Thanks, that was sweet."

For a while, they ate in silence. She stirred the potatoes around the plate before looking up. She drew a labored breath.

"Why did they attack me?"

Jeremy put down his coffee. "Crime of opportunity. You were a defenseless woman who was no match for three strong men. In other words, you were easy prey."

"They said they were going to rape me... but tell me the truth. They were going to kill me afterwards, weren't they?"

Jeremy returned her gaze briefly before brushing his cheeks. His hands were visibly shaking. "They probably would have continued until they got tired of abusing you. Try to forget it. You are safe now, I promise."

She shuddered, nodding slowly as she said, "You told me this town wasn't safe, so I guess you can say 'I told you so'."

He softly replied, "I will never, ever tell you that. I think if you had realized the risk, you might have done things differently. But that's in the past now. How do you feel this morning?"

"My head hurts like hell, especially where that bastard punched me."

Jeremy sat next to her on the bed as he gently examined her eye and face. "I know it hurts, but thankfully I don't see any permanent damage. How about the rest of you?"

"I'm sore all over. Did you see the bruises on my neck?"

He sniffed hard as his lips drew into a little white line. "Yes, I screwed up again."

Her eyes looked to his face. "What?"

Jeremy didn't meet her gaze. "I failed to protect you. I hope in time you'll forgive me."

Protect me? "Forgive you for what?"

"I should've been there."

She was having a hard time understanding his look of sorrow. Her mind shifted from the attack to how he had treated her afterwards. *Like a knight in shining armor, you saved me from hell.* Her eyes searched his face. *You cared for me, not only for my wounds, but also for my soul.* She gulped, "I can't begin to think what would have happened if you hadn't arrived when you did." Her fingers briefly brushed against his cheek. "How did you manage to get there so quickly?"

His face turned red just before he looked away. "I was already looking for you when you answered my call."

Her hand dropped from his cheek. "Looking for me? Why?"

He shifted his weight uncomfortably. "I suspected you would go out for a walk last night. You were still upset over finding out about Britany. But I wasn't quick enough."

"Quick enough for what?"

Hesitation. "To stop you from going out alone."

She shook her head. "No, no! I wanted to be alone. I remember firmly telling you good night."

"Yeah, well, I have lots of flaws. One of them is I don't listen too good. I wanted to make sure you were safe, that's all. Can we drop this?"

The curiosity in her mind demanded an answer. *No, I want to know why you're stalking me again!*

He gave her a half-hearted smile, "Well, I think we can cross this town off the list, what do you think?"

She pulled her long hair out of her eyes, placing her locks behind her ears. She waited until her anger cooled down a little. "We're not moving on just because I was stupid..."

He jumped to his feet as anger filled his eyes. "For heaven's sake! If this town wasn't safe for you, it won't be for our client."

While fuming, she knew he was right. "Conceded, I don't want to stay here, not one minute longer."

"No," he softened, touching her hand. "You should rest today. Then, I think we should take some time off. You need some time to relax, get better, and focus your energy."

She pulled her hand away from him. "Do you have a degree in psychology I don't know about?" She pushed him away as her anger started to boil again. "What gives you the right to tell me what I need to do?"

Jeremy gently took her hands. "Look, when I was in Baghdad, one of my female soldiers was sexually assaulted. I screwed up, sending her right back to duty. As her CO, I should have sent her for some R&R, away from the line. But because she didn't have any physical wounds, I failed to consider the psychological wounds she had suffered."

"I'm not one of your soldiers." Her voice was calmer. "I know you are trying to be nice, but I'm fine."

"You need to be surrounded by people who care for you."

She did a double take. *Don't you care anymore?* "What the hell are you saying?" She pulled her hands from his.

"Look, let's take today off. Tomorrow, I will take you home, where your family can take care of you."

Like hell! She screamed, "And have my family see me like this? What, are you insane?"

"Kaitlin, they'll understand. None of this was your fault."

She searched his eyes as she struggled to breathe calmly. "So I need to be with people who care about me? Isn't that what you just said?"

"Yes," he replied automatically.

Her eyes started to cloud. "I thought I was..." her voice trailed off. "Look, you're not in the damned Army anymore. You don't have some 'duty' to protect me. The way you took care of me last night, from the time we got back into the car until I fell asleep, it sure felt like you cared for me. I could see it in your eyes. What about the way you held me last night, all night long? Can you honestly sit there and tell me you don't care about me?"

"Of course I care," he said, reaching out for her. "We're friends."

Friends! Kaitlin's voice rose with frustration. "Don't be so damned pig-headed!"

He looked away, filling her with sadness. "You need to go back to Chicago. I'll make sure you get there safely."

It was all becoming clear. He was dumping her, just like every man before. *Why is it when I start to really love someone, they decide they don't want me?* She sniffed, "And after that, will you be here waiting for me?"

Again, he looked away, slowly shaking his head. "I'm not a good person. I'm no good for you."

Jumping to her feet, she screamed at him, "You are such an ass. No wonder your wife left you." She ran to the bathroom, slamming the door behind her.

Kaitlin took a long, hot shower. As the water coursed down on her, she loudly ranted. "Damn you, Jeremy Roberts! I hate you. You best be gone when I open that door." The verbalizing of her anger did little to calm her down.

Slowly, her mind drifted back to the way he'd looked into her eyes the night before. She would have sworn she had seen love.

She took her time dressing, afraid of what she would find when she opened the door. Would he still be there? Finally, she could bear it no longer. Slowly, she peeked around the bathroom door. All the lights had been turned off. Silence greeted her.

She was alone, utterly alone. He had gone. She fell to her knees, chest heaving. "Oh, Jeremy, how could you leave me when I needed you?"

Chapter 17

Jeremy jumped as he heard the shower stop. Though he willed them to, his feet hadn't transported him out of the room. *What am I still doing here?* In silence, he prayed for strength. He prayed for wisdom. He prayed for guidance. For the third time since her passing, he heard his mother's voice. *"This girl needs you, Jeremy, more than you can imagine. Be there for her. God will show you how."*

Kaitlin brought him back to the present, He watched her come out of the bathroom and fall to her knees, crying out, "Jeremy, how could you leave me when I needed you?"

He didn't rise at first. His feet still wouldn't let him. For a short eternity, he simply stared at her on the floor. Finally words escaped from his throat, but he didn't know how. "Kaitlin, I didn't leave." He stood and took a cautious step toward her. "I think you need a friend today, and I want to be that friend. I'm here. As long as you want or need me to be."

Kaitlin steadied herself against the television stand and stood, wiping her cheeks. "I-I-I wasn't sure you'd still be here."

Jeremy had no idea what compelled him to say, "Oh ye of little faith. You should have known I would be here.

At least I hope you knew that, didn't you?" *What's happening?* These weren't words he would ever say.

She bounded the few steps across the room and fell into his outstretch arms. They both clung to each other desperately.

"I... I honestly didn't know," she sniffed. "I only hoped you would be. I need you today."

With his arms around her, Jeremy tightened his hug. "I need you, too, much more than you'll ever know."

She pulled back, searching his eyes. "What on earth could you possibly need me for? I'm a mess."

He laughed, "Yes, but you're my mess. How are you feeling?"

Her eyes still showed disbelief. "Pretty spent. How about you?"

His smile was genuine. "Lucky, beyond belief."

They sat, talking about what they should do. Kaitlin conceded that a day of rest would do her good.

Out of nowhere, a thought entered his mind. "Do you like to play games?" he asked.

She eyed him warily, "Please, not the elephant game again."

He chuckled. "All right, we'll leave the elephant in the closet. Maybe board games? Or maybe you'd like to watch TV or go for a movie or something."

Her face lit up as if he had offered her a million dollars. "When I was a girl, every Sunday would be family time. We would play games for hours." Her smile changed from happy to mischievous. "I have to warn you, though, I always win. My sister Kelly used to say they only let me win because I was the baby, but I know that wasn't true."

They sat side by side on the bed, holding hands for the first time in days. Jeremy couldn't begin to express the feelings in his heart. "Tell me about your family."

Somehow, the width of her smile increased. "My home is so full of love. Now mind you, there is a lot of joking and picking on people—mainly me—but it is so wonderful. I can't wait to introduce you to my family."

Introduce me to your family? What did he miss? It's like they fast forwarded a couple of months.

"I have three sisters. Kelly is two years older than me. She's a nurse in Los Angeles. Cassandra is a controller in Savannah and Martina is a lawyer in Chicago." For the next hour, Kaitlin told him about her nieces and nephews and some of the family traditions. He had trouble keeping track of the names, but it seemed like every other person was named Kelly and all three sisters had twins. *Earlier today, I wished I knew more about her and now it's like I struck the lottery!* As an added bonus, getting her to talk about her family took her mind off the assault.

Eventually, she tired. He suggested she should take a nap while he went shopping for a few games and some lunch. *Let's see. She'll want an Italian sub with extra salami, extra mayo, no onions, and barbequed chips. And don't forget the diet Pepsi.* True to his thoughts, that was exactly what she requested. He laughed.

"What's so funny?"

"I knew what you wanted before you told me."

She smirked. "Oh, is that so? Then tell me, Mr. Mind Reader, what else do I want?"

He looked into her eyes. It was so apparent. *A kiss!* But it was too soon. He blushed.

She shot him a million dollar smile, winking. "Ah ha! So you *can* read my mind? I'll have to remember that."

Jeremy used his time wisely, picking out three board games: Scrabble, Trouble, and the Game of Life. He also picked up lunch, and grabbed a bag of golden Oreos and two bottles of chocolate milk for dessert. *It's like I've known her forever.*

She was sleeping when he returned. She looked peaceful and contented, like an angel visiting from Heaven. *Thank you, God, for not allowing me to leave.* Because he hadn't slept the previous night, Jeremy dozed off while he watched her sleep.

The brush of lips light on his forehead brought him out of his slumber. Kaitlin's voice greeted him. "Hey, sleepyhead! Seems the lunch fairy dropped off our food, but..." she wiped her brow with her hand, "...I toiled and slaved over the bag for hours getting it ready for you."

Jeremy couldn't help laughing. She had set the 'table' on the second bed, making even takeout food seem fancy. She patted for him to sit next to her against the headboard. Shyly, she asked, "I usually do this silently, but would you mind if I said grace out loud today?"

His face blushed as he bowed his head. "No, please do."

She reached for his hand, "Heavenly Father, we thank You for this food. Life is sometimes hard, sometimes throwing things at us we hate, things we don't understand. But as always, You never allow us to be alone. You always guide us, always love us, and always give us exactly what we need. Today, I want to ask Your blessing not only on this food, but also on my best friend, Jeremy. Thank You for sending him when You did yesterday. And thank You for bringing him into my life to be my..." she hesitated as she momentarily searched his eyes, "...my friend, my best friend. Please bless our friendship and help us draw closer. Amen." She squeezed his hand extra tightly during the last sentence.

The afternoon was spent in tough board game competition. True to her word, Kaitlin won every single game. She teased him immensely during the Game of Life, asking how many children he wanted stuffed into his car, what he would name them, and interrogating him about his choice of a career. Once again, he sent a prayer to Heaven, but this one of thanks. *God, I don't know what I did to deserve this day, but please don't let it end.*

It was after six when she handed him yet another trouncing in Scrabble. Not only was she smart, but she had excellent strategic skills. Turning to him, she said, "So, soothsayer, read my mind."

He placed his hands to his temple, as if he was actually trying to read her thoughts. "I see many things. But the thing that is most on your mind is... is..." Before he could answer, her lips quickly brushed against his. Opening his eyes in shock, he found her smiling at him.

"You were going to tell me I was hungry," she mocked.

"I, uh, I..."

Her eyes clouded as she took his hands. "Jeremy, today could have been horrible, but just like last night, you knew exactly what I needed. Your stupid—no, not stupid—your nonsensical conversation took my mind off my troubles." She smiled slightly, "I hope I wasn't too forward with the kiss. It was simply a kiss of thanks. But I need to tell you something. When Geeter told me about her—your ex-wife—I felt like you lied to me."

"I wasn't lying, I just..."

She placed her finger against his lips. "Please listen. Apologizing is hard for me. Just before everything went down last night, I finally understood what you meant when you said you wanted to tell me in your own time. I know Britany hurt you. I've been hurt, too. And someday, maybe I will have the courage like you to share my past. Until then, I'd like to see where our special friendship goes. I really care for you, more than I let on. Is that okay?"

Okay? You don't have a clue how much I love you. He would have waited forever, if he thought there was any chance at all. "Yes," he replied breathlessly.

She tickled his ribs. "Okay, smarty. Now read my mind!"

He closed his eyes. *All I can think about is what's on my mind.* He smiled to himself.

She gently smacked his arm, "No, that wasn't it! I'm hungry, Jeremy! You better take me to dinner before I pass out."

***

They ate at a nice Italian restaurant. While waiting for their main course, Kaitlin asked, "So, if we take a couple of days off, where were you thinking we should go?"

Us? Was she serious? "I hadn't thought about it."

"I have. Can we go to San Antonio?"

Anywhere, as long as you're there. "Uh, sure. What's so special about San Antonio?"

Kaitlin smiled across the table. The distance between them seemed to instantly vanish. "Memories."

"Of what?"

She winked. "That's what's so special. I've never been there. We can create all new memories together." She moved her chair close to his and for the rest of the meal, they used her phone to look at potential things to do along the way.

It was almost nine when they returned to her motel room. *I don't want to say good night.*

Kaitlin was eyeing him with a smile that slowly faded. "I don't know exactly how to say this, so I'll just blurt it out. I'm still a little scared to stay by myself."

Jeremy smiled sadly. Despite the wonderful day, the memories of her trauma would last for a long time. He squeezed her hands firmly.

Her eyes were bright as she continued. "Now, I don't want you to get the wrong impression because I'm not

94

that kind of girl," she went on, "but I want a repeat of last night."

Jeremy's mouth dropped open. "You were assaulted last night."

She blushed. "Not that part. I want you to hold me again while I fall asleep. Would you mind?"

In disbelief, he asked, "Are you sure?"

She slowly nodded. "It was the best night's sleep I ever had. It felt so safe with you by my side. Realize, this isn't a come on. I don't want to make love. I need, well, I want you to hold me. Would you, please?"

In less than a nanosecond, he softly replied, "Yes."

He couldn't believe the width of her smile. "Give me a few minutes to get dressed."

While she changed, Jeremy ran to his room. As he went through his duffel bag, he realized he hadn't even slept in his bed. *I must be dreaming. God, please don't let me wake up to find this is just a beautiful dream.*

He arrived back at her room, wondering what she would wear. Again, she had sweats on. The bedcovers had been rolled back. She climbed in first before Jeremy turned off the lights.

Kaitlin was there waiting for him, taking him into her arms this time. He felt her nose against his. "Jeremy, I said something earlier I want to take back."

Panic started to fill his mind. *Please don't let our closeness fade away!*

Her hair was tickling his nose. "I want you to," she hesitated, "I want you to call me Katie. Kaitlin is your co-worker," again, she hesitated, "But I'm Katie, your," her voice grew silent for a moment, "your best friend." Unexpectedly, her lips softly touched his.

Jeremy's arms wrapped around her. A sigh of contentment escaped past their joined lips. He had fantasized about kissing her from day one, but those dreams were pale comparisons to the reality. The kiss was slow, sensual and long.

Afterwards, she placed her head on his shoulder. "Goodnight, Jeremy."

This is what Heaven must feel like. "Good night, Katie." *I love you!*

Chapter 18

Kaitlin stared at the man lying next to her. A few short hours ago, she could have pictured herself waking up next to him until the day she died; not now. She still couldn't believe what he said as he slept. *You are the stupidest woman ever to have lived!*

Jeremy started to stir. She had decided that when they got close to an airport, she would tell him she had changed her mind. She was going back to Chicago, where people who *really* loved her would be waiting.

His eyes slowly opened as a smile spread across his face. He reached to kiss her lips. She turned her head, allowing him only to graze her cheek.

"How is my Katie this morning?"

Your Katie? Fat chance!

She forced a smile. "I'm fine. Sleep well?"

"Best ever!" He studied her face, his smile leaving. "What's wrong?"

"Nothing," she said, rolling out of bed. "I'm going to grab a shower."

She had tried her best to keep her feelings hidden, yet he gently touched her shoulder as if he could read her mind. "Did I do something wrong?"

You let your true colors show! "Nope."

"Then what's wrong? I feel like you have buyer's remorse or something? We were so close last night."

She looked in his direction but didn't make eye contact. "No, it's not like that. Well, maybe we moved a little too fast last night. Everything happened much faster than I wanted it to."

His mouth dropped open. "I-I'm sorry. I thought you *wanted* to sleep together. What did I do wrong? Did I snore or something?"

She still couldn't look at his eyes. "I'm not sure this was such a good idea."

"What wasn't a good idea? Us?"

Her face was tortured. *Allowing myself to fall in love with you. How could I be so stupid?* "Yes, I mean no, I mean the whole idea of us being involved and working together isn't a good idea."

Jeremy jumped out of bed, grabbing his cell phone.

What the...? "Who are you calling?"

"Human Resources."

You wouldn't dare! Fear ran up and down her spine. "Why? You are *not* going to tell them about us or what happened, are you?"

He looked at her with a puzzled expression, "What's between us is only between us. No one will ever know what happened in this town unless you tell them." Then his mouth dropped into a frown. "No, I am quitting my job." As Kaitlin stared in disbelief, he held up a finger and spoke into the phone, "Jenny? Hi. It's Jeremy Roberts. Wow, you're in early. How are you doing?" Kaitlin's mouth dropped. She couldn't believe he'd actually called the Tower. "Great, and how are those children of yours? Oh, good. Could you please connect me to HR's voicemail? Thanks."

"What do you think you're doing?" Kaitlin whispered harshly.

Jeremy held his hand over the bottom of the phone. "If the two of us being involved and working together is an issue, I'll quit. So I can be with you."

Her mind started racing in circles. All her experience with men—and what Jeremy had murmured while he slept—were telling her to run. When he eventually got what he wanted from her, he would surely drop the romance. It was only a matter of time.

"Hi Deb, this is Jeremy Roberts," she heard him say into the phone. "Would you mind returning my phone call at your earliest convenience? Thank you and I look forward to speaking with you."

Kaitlin stood facing him, hands on her hips. "What are you trying to pull?"

A look of determination was in his eyes. "I just told you. If it comes down to a choice between work and you, work will lose, every... single... time."

She stared in disbelief. "Come off it. This is some game you are playing."

"I don't play games, not when it comes to you. Time out for a second, okay?"

She took a deep breath, nodding.

"Just close your eyes," he said, smiling gently. "I want you to picture something. I want you to remember how close we were last night. And remember when we looked up at the North Star a couple of days ago, and how we said we would let it guide us? What do you see?"

He was at it again! How could he send her into a trance with only his words? "I'm not going to play this game with you." She shook her head as if to break the spell. "I'm heading into the shower. I'll be ready in twenty minutes."

He stood there silent and still.

Damn you, Jeremy! As she looked back, she realized she'd loved him since the day they met at the Tower. She couldn't make it into the bathroom quick enough.

He was gone by the time she came out, which was good. It would take her a while to pack.

As soon as they loaded up the Suburban, Kaitlin plugged in her headset, staring out the window with watery eyes. After the closeness of the previous day, the silence and distance between them was unbearable. She was filled with despair. For two and a half hours, they drove without uttering a syllable.

Finally, Jeremy pulled into the Alabama Welcome Center on Interstate 65 a little outside of Chattanooga, Tennessee. Kaitlin started to get out, thinking it was a restroom break, until he gently touched her arm.

His face was pale as he said, "Kaitlin, please talk to me. If I did something wrong, I apologize. But I can't take this roller coaster of emotions."

This is your fault, not mine. She didn't want to look in his eyes, so she studied her fingernails instead. "I really don't have anything to say."

"I find that hard to believe after our talk yesterday," he smiled.

"Well, that's a mistake I won't ever make again," she growled.

His expression looked as if he had lost everything he cared for. "Please Katie, I care about you so much but I don't understand."

She looked away. *You're such a great liar.* "Don't understand what?"

His hands were trembling. "What happened since last night? We were so close. I can't take this."

What if... She turned in the seat to face him, "Do you really want to know what's wrong?"

"More than anything," he replied, his voice cracking.

All right. You want to play this game, let's do it! Looking directly into his eyes, she asked, "Then answer my question."

"Anything, just ask."

Can you look me in the eyes and lie to me? She hesitated for a second, watching for the slightest sign of deceit. "Did you have any dreams last night?"

He took a moment to think before answering, but his eyes never left hers. "Yes, a nightmare."

Her hand flew out and slapped him. "You bastard! Yesterday was a nightmare to you? I invited you into my bed." She was having trouble getting her breath. Pain started deep within her chest, almost as if her heart was being ripped out. She raised her hand to slap him a second time.

Jeremy gently grasped her hands, "I wasn't finished. I dreamed about my wedding day with Brit. We had just said our vows, but when I got to the back of the church, she was gone. I searched for her, calling her name, only to find her in another man's arms. I walked away in disgust but suddenly, you were there. That's when my nightmare turned into a dream, a great dream. I said, 'Oh honey, I've been looking for you,' then I told you I loved you over and over and over again." He was blushing.

Now Kaitlin was totally confused. She dropped her hand to her lap. *Are you that good of a liar or are you serious?* She stared at him, in shock. "You talk in your sleep. What woke me was when I heard you calling her name. I turned the light on, watching your face. It looked like you were in pain, but then it brightened when I heard you keep repeating, 'I love you.' For once in your life, be honest, who were you really saying 'I love you' to? Britany? Or me?"

His blush deepened. "I said it to you."

Sarcasm dripped from her voice. "Really? Sure you're not covering your tracks? You have a habit of lying to me."

"Lying to you? Why is it you always expect the worst from me?"

"Your track record speaks for itself."

"My track record? What the hell?"

"You called her name, then said, 'I love you, I love you, I love you.' What am I supposed to think?"

"How about believing what I told you. Is that so hard to do?"

"Just tell me the truth."

He slammed his hands against the steering wheel. "Dammit, I did. It was *you* I said it to. How could you even suspect... Haven't you been paying attention? Think back to how I've treated you. If my love hasn't shown through, it never will. I can't believe this." His lips were white as he gritted his teeth together.

It wasn't his words, but rather how he said them that caught her attention. *Could this be the truth?* She didn't know what to think. "Well, now you know my confusion. You already told me when you love someone, truly love someone, it never ends. You told me you don't want to be with her, yet there you were holding me, but calling her name and repeating 'I love you.' What would you think if the role was reversed?" Her eyes became scratchy. "Men have used me before. I will not allow it again." *I love you, but I won't go through this for you or any man!*

The ringing of his cell phone interrupted them. He glanced at it momentarily before silencing it. *Who are you avoiding?* She grabbed the phone from his hand, immediately recognizing the number for GDC's office. *Damn you! You lied to me again!* Everything he said this morning had been a lie! She taunted him, "Jeremy, it's the Tower calling."

He glared at her.

Anger rose in her throat as she taunted him even more. "What, did you change your mind? I thought you were going to quit if it meant something coming between us. I don't mean anything to you, do I? You really don't care. It was all a lie, wasn't it?" *You never loved me, did you?* Despite her anger, her heart was breaking.

Jeremy's eyes shone brightly with rage as he grabbed his phone back. "Jeremy Roberts. Oh, hi Deb. I only called to ask a simple question about my employment. If I decide to leave the company, how do I go about it? Yes, you heard me correctly!"

Kaitlin's mouth dropped open. He was serious! *No you don't.* If he quit, she was screwed. Any chance of promotion or success would be gone. She ripped the phone from his hand, "Debbie? This is Kaitlin Jenkins. Please ignore Jeremy. We were arguing about the last town. No, he doesn't mean it. Yes, I will convince him otherwise. Yes, I agree, we couldn't finish this project without him, I know that. I will try to talk some sense into him. Please disregard his call this morning. Just forget it ever happened. Of course, I will be glad to put him back on." She placed her hand over the phone, pointing her finger at his face, "You made your point. Don't you dare quit on me."

He took the phone, supporting her lie to their employer. He explained that they disagreed over how to score the last town they were in. It took him fifteen minutes to convince Deb he had jumped the gun. He apologized, saying he was wrong for bothering her. He thanked her for her time before ending the call.

Kaitlin looked at him, not fully understanding. *Who are you, really?* Her heart was still hurting over what he said as he slept. She shook her head, "Well, either you are a true gem or the slickest liar I ever met. Right now, I'm not really sure which one. Maybe you set up something with my attackers to gain my trust to get me into bed? Is that it?" As soon as she said it, she wished she could take it back.

His face turned bright red as his eyes welled with tears. *Oh my God! I crossed the line.* She was pretty sure his anger wasn't because she had figured him out. He didn't bother to answer. He exited the Suburban, slamming the door so hard the entire vehicle shook. He stormed off to the Welcome Center.

She knew she had made a capital mistake. She started to follow him. "Come back here, please," she pleaded, "that was wrong of me." He ignored her as he walked away.

You stupid idiot! She placed her head in her hands.

She spoke softly, just to hear a noise. "Why did I say that? He rescued me! They cut him with a knife and he didn't care, instead, he was more concerned about me." As she was waiting for his return, she whispered, "I really love him, but..." A horrible thought entered her mind. "Please don't let this be the end, please, please! He's not like the others. It's only that..." Then the truth dawned on her...

Chapter 19

*I*t was twenty minutes before Jeremy returned to climb into the Suburban. His eyes were red as he pointed the SUV onto Interstate 65 south. It was his turn to be silent. *I'm done.*

Chattanooga was fifty miles behind them when Kaitlin asked, "Can we talk?"

He didn't answer, nor did he look at her.

She waited a few seconds before speaking. "I'm sorry. What I said was so wrong. Can you forgive me?"

I am nothing to you.

Again, he was silent as he concentrated on driving.

"Every other man in my life only wanted one thing."

He scoffed, "Yeah, well, I'm not them."

"I know, it's just—"

"Congratulations," he interrupted, his voice cracking. "You did something not even Britany could do."

"What's that?" she asked, almost begging.

Between the tears and his anger, he was about to boil over. "I have been nothing but kind to you, but you could care less. Everything you've done has been like a knife in the back."

"Let me explain..."

Again, he interrupted, "If I'd wanted to take advantage of you, don't you think I would have tried last night?" *I thought you were the one.*

"Jeremy, I didn't..."

"I wanted it to be beautiful. But you? You think all I want is sex."

She was silent.

He glanced from the road to her face. "No, I wanted something much more with you. I wanted us to have a fairy tale love story."

Her face blanched as he watched his words slowly sink into her heart. "A love story? You mean..."

"I didn't realize you thought so little of me!"

She whispered, "Forgive me."

"Did you really believe... Oh, just forget it!" *It's over.*

He yanked his cell from his pocket, speaking into it, "Directions to the closest recruiting station."

Kaitlin's face paled even further. "W-w-what are you doing?"

The device's voice asked, "Which recruiting station would you like?"

Jeremy glared at Kaitlin. "I'm going back to where I'm wanted," he said, then spoke into the phone again. "Army."

Kaitlin ripped the device from his hand, yelling into it, "Stop navigation."

The device replied, "We don't appear to be navigating anywhere."

Kaitlin fumed, "Oh we're going somewhere, just not the right place." To Jeremy she begged, "Would you please pull the car over?"

Here? Jeremy stared at her, "Why, what's wrong?"

"I need you to pull over," she insisted.

In the middle of nowhere? "Are you sick?"

She slammed her hand against the dash, raising her voice. "Pull the damned car over now!"

He obeyed.

She turned, looking at his face. "I listened to you. Now it's your turn to listen."

Great, another fight. No, our last fight. He made himself comfortable. "It's a free country, go ahead."

Quietly she replied, "Suppose you said something you really regretted and wish you could take it back, something that hurt someone you care for. How would you ask for forgiveness and explain you made a big mistake?"

How about not saying it in the first place? "It doesn't matter anymore."

She reached over to touch his hand. "Yes, yes it does."

He remained quiet until his anger had dissipated. "I would ask for forgiveness. And prove it by being open and honest about my true feelings."

She pondered his response for a few seconds then asked him to get out of the vehicle with her.

He sighed loudly, but did, walking around to where she stood. She took both of his hands and started to kneel.

He shook his head as he lifted her up. "You don't have to do this. I forgive you."

"No, I need to." She again took a knee, looking up at him.

I won't let you. He lifted her up a second time, softly but forcibly saying, "No!"

She shook her head. "No one has ever cared for me like you do. I'm not good at this whole romance thing. It is so hard for me to trust any man," she hesitated to search his face, "but I do trust you."

He scoffed, "Yeah, right. Somehow, I'm having trouble believing that."

"Look, I screwed up. What I said had less to do with you than with my past. Please forgive me. I promise I will never take your feelings or actions for granted again."

Jeremy had been looking at the ground while she spoke. She grabbed his chin so his eyes gazed into hers. "I have never truly been in love, but I can tell you, the feelings you brought out in me are strong. Is it love? Maybe, I hope so, I want it to be more than anything, yet I don't know, not yet. You have become the friend I always wanted, the one I dreamed of, the one I always prayed would come."

She stopped to push her bangs out of her eyes.

"I know you were hurt by Britany; I know I hurt you, too. I can't guarantee I won't make mistakes, but I promise you that it will never be intentional. Please forgive me. I don't want to have thrown away the best gift God ever sent my way." Tears were forming at the corners of her hazel eyes until one slowly dribbled out.

Don't cry. I can't take that.

Her eyes pleaded as much as her words, "Is there any way we can we pick up where we left off?"

Unconsciously, he trembled momentarily. "I want that, too, but I can't take the constant swings of emotion."

Kaitlin nodded vigorously. "I will try my hardest... if you do one thing in return."

He smiled, "Always something with you, isn't it?"

She gently punched his arm. "Smarty!" Her smile left as she grabbed his hands. "Please don't keep secrets from me."

A lock of hair had drifted back over her left eye. He brushed it away. "I promise. But if I'm not clear on something, you need to ask before jumping to conclusions. Deal?" He held out his hand.

Kaitlin instead hugged him tighter than ever. He held her for a few seconds before pulling away enough to look into those eyes. "You don't want any secrets between us, do you?"

She whispered, "No."

"Then I need to tell you something. I love you... more than I loved anyone," he kissed her fingers, "including Britany."

Kaitlin's breath came rapidly. She peered intently at his eyes. "There's something important I need to tell you, too."

Chapter 20

*J*eremy realized the Fourth of July holiday was only a few days away and Kaitlin wanted to spend it with family. And him! Her parents were in Scotland, and her sister Kelly's clan was in Hawaii. That left her sister Cassandra in Savannah, who had graciously invited them to stay.

After finishing the assessment on Friday, Kaitlin e-mailed her report to the Tower while Jeremy packed up the Suburban. They were on the road by one. Heading down the interstate, she rested her head against his shoulder. Her fingers traced the outline of his as she held his hand.

He smiled at the warmth. "Tell me about Cassandra and her family."

She kissed his hand before leaning back in the seat so she could see his face. "She's my oldest sister."

"Refresh my memory. You have three sisters, right?"

"Yep, Cassie's the oldest, followed by Martina, then Kelly. Cassandra and Martina had a different father. Their father died when they were young, and mom remarried. Of course, I'm the baby of the family."

"My favorite one," he interjected with a smile that crinkled his face, "in case you didn't know."

"I suspected as much." They exchanged a look which ended in a quick kiss. She leaned against his shoulder and snuggled with him as they drove.

"My sisters are great. Cassandra is a controller for Coca-Cola. She and her husband John have six kids, ranging from seventeen years old down to five."

"Wow, that's a huge spread. If they're anything like you, they'll be wonderful."

His compliment brought a smile to her lips. But her smile quickly turned into a frown. "I'm nervous. She's the naysayer of the family. You're the first man I've ever brought to meet anyone in my family. I just hope she doesn't bring up my past."

He squeezed her hand, saying, "And if she does, so what? You and I, our love is strong."

Kaitlin sat up so she could see his face. "I agree. Do you think we're going too fast?"

With a reassuring smile, he winked at her. "Well, the last couple of weeks have been like a rocket sled, but as for me, I'm happier than ever before. And you? You are perfect."

Her smile split her face from ear to ear. "I don't see me like you do. In my eyes, I'm only a plain, average girl."

He frowned. "No. You're so much more than that. I don't compliment you to make you feel good. I say the things I do because that's what I feel. I love you, forever. We were meant to be."

***

Kaitlin directed Jeremy into the driveway of the Lucia residence around supper time. The gigantic old house had a full wraparound porch. The landscaping was gorgeous with thousands of flowers in bloom. A boy with thick glasses was playing basketball by himself. Jeremy exited the Suburban and held the door open for Kaitlin. She murmured a quick prayer.

The little boy continued to shoot baskets while his parents came outside. The sisters hugged and John shook Jeremy's hand. Kaitlin pulled Jeremy over to introduce her nephew Kevin, before following her sister inside.

"I've heard a lot about you, Kevin," Jeremy said, extending his hand.

Kevin pushed his thick glasses back up his nose and shook Jeremy's hand. "So, are you going to marry Aunt Katie?"

Jeremy blushed, stuttering, "I-I-I don't know. I haven't asked her yet."

"She's the only one besides Ellie who likes me."

"Ellie?"

"My older sister. The one with pink hair."

Jeremy nodded. "Oh, I see. Want to play ball together?"

"Sure," Kevin said, smiling for the first time. He tossed the ball to Jeremy and they played until Cassandra called them to supper.

By the time they went inside, the two had become fast friends. Kevin wanted Jeremy to sit next to him, so Kaitlin changed her seat to sit on the other side of Jeremy. During the prayer, she squeezed his hand under the table.

As they ate their fried chicken, the conversation was all about the exploits of the kids. After a while Cassandra said, "So Jeremy, Kaitlin never mentioned a word about you until this week. How long have you known each other?"

Jeremy was prepared. "We met in March at work. We've become very close friends."

Kevin chimed in, "Yes, but Mr. Jeremy hasn't asked Aunt Katie to marry him yet!" This brought loud laughter, and for two people, bright red faces.

Cassandra, however, gave Kaitlin a stern look. "Don't tell me you're this serious after such a short period of time."

Kaitlin almost choked on her lima beans. "Uh, no." She glanced at Jeremy. "Not yet." They hadn't openly discussed marriage, though it had crossed her mind. She couldn't read his thoughts, but a mischievous smile covered his face as he winked at her. It made her heart fill with happiness.

"Yet?" Cassandra repeated, bringing Kaitlin back to earth.

It suddenly became extremely hot at the table. "Can we change the subject?"

"You don't have a good history with men, and someone has to watch out for you," her sister huffed.

John shook his head, "Cassie..."

Cassandra cut the legs out from under her husband, "I have a right to do this. The first three men..."

Jeremy interjected, "That would be Billy, Craig, and Ronny. Honestly, they were not men. I know all about them and what happened. I also know none of it was your sister's fault. Don't judge her."

The room filled with silence. Cassandra looked ready to explode. Every other pair of eyes watched Jeremy.

"Sorry," he said. "I didn't mean to be disrespectful in your home, but please don't talk down to Katie. She doesn't deserve that."

The uneasy silence continued until one of the five-year-old twins asked, "Aunt Katie, can I play games on your phone?"

Katie welcomed the break from the tension. Turning to her niece, she said, "I think you mean 'May I?'"

"*May I* play games on your phone?" the twin repeated.

Kaitlin smiled again. "Yes, you may." She unlocked her phone and handed it to her niece. The twins left the table together.

John turned toward Jeremy. "Katie tells us you were in the Army."

"Yes, sir. Captain in the Rangers."

"Rangers? Did you see action?"

"Yeah, quite a bit. Four tours in Iraq and three in Afghanistan. Retired as an instructor at Fort Benning."

"Did you kill anyone?" Kevin asked excitedly.

Cassandra's eyes shot daggers, "Kevin! That type of talk is not appropriate!"

After dinner, Jeremy headed out to play ball with Kevin and the rest of the males, while Kaitlin and Cassandra cleaned up the dinner dishes.

"How serious are the two of you?" Cassandra asked pointedly.

Kaitlin had been dreading this conversation, primarily because she didn't expect it to go well. "Cassie, this is the first time I have really been in love. He saved me." She told her about the assault, the rescue, his care afterwards, and an abridged version of their romance. "He might be the one. Please don't take a stand against him."

Her older sister's face softened. "That must have been horrible," she said, reaching out to hug Kaitlin. "I'm glad you're okay. As far as trying to stand between you, I won't. I just don't want to see you get hurt again."

"He's not like the others. Some mornings I have to pinch myself to see if this is real."

Cassandra started to say something when Jeremy came in.

"I forgot how quick teenagers could move. I sure could use a shower, if you'd be willing to point me in the right direction," he said. Cassandra laughed and provided him with a towel, directing him to the guest bathroom. Through the walls, they could hear Jeremy singing Hank Snow's 'Hello, Love.'

As Kaitlin drained the sink and Cassandra put away the last dish, her oldest twin came in. "Aunt Katie, why do you have a naked picture of Mr. Jeremy on your phone?"

Kaitlin's mouth dropped open. "What?"

Cassandra grabbed Kaitlin's arm, displeasure showing in her face. "You have a naked picture of him on your phone and you gave it to my girls?"

She ignored her sister. Her niece was pointing at the next room, "Ellie found it."

"Where's my phone?" Kaitlin yelped, her ears turning red.

The twin continued to point to the next room. "Ellie has it."

Kaitlin ran in to where Ellie was sitting, playing with her pink hair while going through the phone. Grabbing the phone from her niece's hand, Kaitlin screamed at her, "What were you thinking? How dare you go through my photos?"

Ellie gave her a surly look. "Get a life, Aunt Katie. He's really cute naked."

Kaitlin scanned her phone and to her horror, discovered that Ellie had texted the picture and the words 'My new boyfriend' to the entire extended family. To her further surprise, the response from Martina said, "You lucky girl!" and from Kelly, "You little horn dog! Congrats! ☺" Her mother had simply replied, "Call me NOW!"

Then to her surprise, a new text came in. Cassandra had replied, "Good heavens. You naughty girl. I hope your relationship is NOT based on what I see in this photo."

***

Jeremy walked into the room, "Hey gorgeous!" He stopped in his tracks when he caught the look on Kaitlin's face. "What's wrong? Are you still upset by what I said to your sister?"

Kaitlin was fighting back tears. Grabbing him by the arm, she dragged him outside.

Away from the house she finally turned. In the moonlight, he could see the tracks of tears on her face.

"I know this will end us. I'm s-s-s-sorry. I didn't mean it."

"What are you talking about?" he said, wiping her cheeks gently.

Jeremy could sense her feeling of panic. "I never should have taken the picture in the first place, but I didn't think Ellie would..."

"What picture?"

She looked away. "The one I took in San Antonio. The shower picture."

Jeremy's face turned white. "When I was naked?" She nodded. "I thought we agreed to delete those pictures."

Kaitlin dropped her head. "I know, but I saved one. Just one."

His shock turned to anger. "Dammit!"

"I know, but..."

Closing his eyes, he forced himself to calm down. His voice was soft as he spoke. "So who saw it?"

"Ellie." Kaitlin buried her head in her hands. "But the worst thing is... the worst thing is she sent it to everyone in my family."

Jeremy stared at her for a few seconds before letting out a long guffaw. "For a moment, I thought you were serious!"

She dropped her hands to look directly at him and the look on her face told him she wasn't joking. Kaitlin held her phone out to him. "Here, look!"

His frivolity left as he glanced at her text message display, then walked away. He sat on the grass and dropped his head. *They'll hate me! Think I'm some pervert.*

Kaitlin sank down next to him and put a hand on his knee. "I apologize. I never intended for anyone besides me to see it."

"Too late for that now." He looked up at the stars. "Remember when I said we could always look to the North Star for guidance? I am getting nothing."

"I'm sorry," she repeated.

He quickly turned to her. "Talk about a first impression! Your family will hate me."

"I never once in a million years..."

He grabbed her, pulling her onto his lap. "Understand this. I love you and no matter what happens, we won't allow anything to come between us."

Kaitlin stopped sobbing, and looked at him with puzzlement. "You're not mad?"

"Hell yes, I'm mad. But not at you. At Ellie. How could she violate your privacy like that?"

Her eyes were wide as she stared at him. "Y-y-you're not mad at me? I was afraid you would get in the car and leave."

Determination was in his face. "What? Never. Not in a million years. There's damned little you could ever do to make me leave you." *Don't you realize how much I love you?* He cupped her chin in his hands. "God, this must be horrible for you. How do you feel?"

Her mouth dropped in shock. "Me? Your naked picture is being circulated and you're concerned about me?"

He raised his eyebrows. "I can't do anything about that now. I refuse to let it come between us, *ever*. But how do you think your family will react?"

Kaitlin smiled as she wiped her cheeks, "Well, honestly, you're getting rave reviews. Even my grandma wants to meet you!"

Chapter 21

Kaitlin noted the house was subdued when they returned. Ellie's parents had grounded her until long after college graduation. The rest of the kids were already in bed.

Jeremy carried in their luggage and set it at the base of the stairs. "Where do you want us to sleep?" he asked Cassandra.

"Kaitlin can sleep in Tommy's room and I laid out a sleeping bag for you in the den downstairs." Kaitlin turned to look at Jeremy. He smiled sadly and shrugged his shoulders.

John grabbed Kaitlin's matching bags, heading upstairs. Jeremy picked up his duffel, preparing to follow Cassandra.

"No! This is unacceptable." Kaitlin objected loudly, *I can't get to sleep without his arms around me.* "Sis, I am an adult. Jeremy sleeps with me."

Cassandra turned and looked at her sternly. "In case you haven't noticed, we have children in this house! It's bad enough you bring pornographic photos into my home and now you want to sleep with him?"

"If your daughter hadn't nosed around on my phone, she wouldn't have seen them."

"What do you expect children to do with a phone?"

Jeremy interrupted. "Ladies, let's calm down. Cassandra, we'll honor your wishes. I'll just sleep—"

Kaitlin whipped around to face Jeremy. "Don't you dare wimp out on me! I know you want to sleep with me just as much as I want to sleep with you. We sleep together, end of the conversation. Either here or somewhere else. Turning back to her sister, she said, "We can go to a motel if we have to. So which is it, Cassie? Should we stay or go?"

Cassandra looked uncomfortable, but John answered for her, "We respect you, and of course you are an adult. Here, let me show you both to Tommy's room."

Cassandra shot her husband a look that implied there would be further conversation behind closed doors.

Later, in their room, Katie again apologized, but Jeremy laughed it off. He hugged her and shushed away her fears.

Tommy had a full-sized bed, which was much smaller than the queen- and king-sized beds they were accustomed to in the motels.

They awoke before the kids and came downstairs. Cassandra and John were already enjoying a morning cup of coffee.

"Good morning, you two," John greeted them. With merriment in his eyes he asked, "So how did you sleep..." pausing for a moment before adding, "...big guy?" He managed to get it out before bursting into laughter.

Cassandra blushed, "John!" But the rest of their laughter drowned her out.

John extended his hand, "Welcome to the family."

Breakfast was a blur, except for Ellie's entrance with her head down. She didn't make eye contact, but said, "Mr. Jeremy, I'm sorry for texting your photo. I shouldn't have done that."

He walked over, lifting her chin with his finger so they could see eye to eye. Nodding, he replied, "I accept your apology, Ellie. Everyone makes mistakes and has regrets. I forgive you, so with me, forget it. But you owe Aunt Katie a bigger apology. You had no right to look through her photos without her consent. Texting personal information to others was a very mean thing to do. Do you understand that?"

Her dark brown eyes were wet. "Yes, sir." She turned to face Kaitlin. "Aunt Katie, I'm really sorry."

Kaitlin looked angry for a moment before her face sadly smiled. *If Jeremy can forgive you, I can, too.* "Like Jeremy said, everyone makes mistakes. I forgive you." She was the eldest and was probably lost in this big family. *I know you didn't mean any harm. Only a cry for attention.*

To everyone's surprise, Jeremy turned suddenly to face John and Cassandra. "Mom and Dad, on behalf of Ellie, I would ask if you could lift her grounding just for today so she can come along on our trip to Savannah. I don't want anyone to be excluded. However, you are her parents and I understand your punishment, but..." He knelt before them, begging with his hands clasped, "Please, with a cherry on top?"

Cassandra and John exchanged a look of disbelief that ended in laughter. "If you two can forgive her, we can too," John answered, "but we'll have a long discussion about it later. Get dressed, Ellie, because everyone else is ready to go."

Ellie gave Jeremy a quick embrace, then turned to her aunt for an extra-long hug, "I'm really sorry. I'll never do that again. I learned my lesson."

Kaitlin brushed the hair from Ellie's eyes. "It's okay. Hurry and get dressed."

All ten of them piled into the Suburban while Kaitlin drove. She noticed Jeremy in the rearview mirror, looking so happy.

Cassandra directed them down to the shore to do a family photograph. Jeremy volunteered to take the photo, but Cassandra insisted he be in the picture. "You're family now. Get in the photo." She grabbed his hand and said, "Wait." Both Kaitlin and Jeremy turned to stare at her. She looked him over from head to toe.

"What's wrong," Kaitlin asked.

Cassandra started giggling, "Just wanted to make sure he was fully dressed before we took it." A passerby took the picture for them.

As they started back to the Suburban, Cassandra said, "Jeremy, may I have a word with you?"

Kaitlin wrapped her arm around his waist.

Jeremy looked over and said, "I'll catch up with you in a minute, sweetheart."

Kaitlin shook her head. "I'll stay."

"Can you believe this, Jeremy? My sister doesn't trust me," Cassandra laughed.

Kaitlin didn't move.

Cassandra shook her head. "It's okay, Katie. I'm on your side." She touched her younger sister's face before turning to Jeremy. "I owe you an apology. I was afraid Katie made a bad choice. But she told me what you did for her. Thank you."

He smiled, "My pleasure."

Cassandra also smiled. "And the way you smoothed over Ellie's faux pas was so wonderful for her. I believe that made more of an impression than grounding her for three years. I'll admit, my initial impression of you was wrong. Can you forgive me for judging you incorrectly?"

Jeremy glanced at Kaitlin. She shot him a wink. "Nothing to forgive," he said, reaching for Kaitlin's hand. "I love your sister, very much. She's what I've been searching for my entire life." The three of them stared at each other momentarily, until Kaitlin started laughing.

"Hey, wait! You're just apologizing because you saw Jeremy's photo, aren't you?"

Cassandra and Jeremy joined her laughter, and Cassandra gave her a quick hug. "No, of course not. But you do realize, our family will tease the two of you about this forever and a day, right?"

Chapter 22

*J*eremy smiled as he watched Kaitlin drive them around. *Do you know I want you forever?* His train of thought was broken by Cassandra, "We were planning on a family game night tonight, but the country club is holding a ball. We can have our game time tomorrow morning, but maybe the two of you would like to join us at the dance?"

Kaitlin looked at him in the mirror with hope. *You want to go, don't you, sweetheart?* "That would be wonderful," Jeremy said. "There is one problem, though."

"What's that?" Cassandra responded.

"I don't have any dress clothes. Kaitlin probably does in one of those hundred suitcases." He was glad he wasn't next to her, because she waved a fist at him before laughing.

"We could stop at the mall," Cassandra said. "I'm sure no matter how many clothes Kaitlin might have toted along, she won't mind shopping for something new."

From the driver's seat, Kaitlin said, "What Cassie is really saying is she wants some sister bonding time shopping with me."

"Girls call it retail therapy," John chimed in. "But I'll take the boys with me, if you ladies want to shop. We'll check out Dick's Sporting Goods. Maybe as part of her punishment, Ellie should take the twins to the playground at the mall."

Jeremy smiled. "I see one, no make that two problems."

"What's that, honey?" Kaitlin asked.

"If we split like that, I'll be alone, and you know how men shop... I might come back with purple Spandex pants, a yellow golf shirt, and a forest green tie. I think I need some female input. Maybe Ellie and I could take the twins, and she could help me pick out something nice before we hit the kid's place. Thoughts?" *The girl already learned her lesson. I want to see her included.*

"I would love that, Mr. Jeremy," Ellie exclaimed, "but I think hot pink Spandex would go better with your eyes!" Everyone laughed. "May I go with him, Mom and Dad, please? He needs my help!"

After a brief discussion, her parents consented.

Ellie turned to smile at him. Jeremy could feel Kaitlin's loving eyes watching him in the mirror. "Ellie, drop mister. I am simply Jeremy, okay?"

Kaitlin shot him a wink and Jeremy blew a kiss in return.

Ellie was still watching him, smiling. He was glad he had smoothed everything over, even asking for her help. The poor kid needed a break. As the oldest child, she probably had it tougher than the rest of her siblings. *I believe you and I have a lot in common, kid!*

Kaitlin shook her head as she watched the silent exchange. "What's the second problem?"

"First I need to know what you'll be wearing. Any idea what color dress you will pick?" *Short and silky would work for me...*

"I'll have to see what they have down here. Can I call you when I pick something out?"

"Why don't you text me a photo of it so Ellie can help me pick out the color of the shirt? Just make sure you text the right photo, one with clothes in it." They both shared another wink simultaneously.

At the mall, Jeremy hoisted a twin in each arm before kissing Kaitlin goodbye. Ellie had quite the eye for fashion, and soon he had purchased a stunning black suit. They took the twins to the playground while waiting for Kaitlin's text.

"So, Ellie, what do you want to do after high school?"

Ellie turned to him with a smile so wide he could see her braces. "I want to see Europe. Been saving every penny so I can go. London, Paris, Barcelona."

Just be careful, kid. "Then what?"

"I want to be a marine biologist, you know, like maybe a dolphin trainer. I love water and everything that lives in it." Ellie opened up to him as she shared her dreams. *I'm glad her parents let her come.* She was a sweet kid. Probably a lot like Katie was as a child.

Forgiveness was one of the many life's lessons his parents had instilled in him. *Be slow to anger and quick to forgive, Dad always said.* Jeremy was thankful he'd forgiven Ellie. Spending time with Kaitlin's tribe reminded him how much he missed being part of a real family; the Army had been his family for fourteen years, but it never replaced his mom and dad. *This is what I've been missing.*

The twins played on the trampoline for about twenty minutes before Kaitlin texted. "My dress is black with red highlights. Can't wait to model it for you in person. Photo attached. TTFN!"

He texted back, "TTFN? Take time for naughtiness? Katie! Suppose one of the kids reads this?"

"No, silly! Ta-ta for now. You know, from Winnie the Pooh?"

He laughed and Ellie asked what was so funny. Bringing up the text and photo, he showed the dress to Ellie. After collecting the twins, they headed back to the men's clothing store and Ellie helped him pick out a dark red shirt and a black tie that had Winnie the Pooh embroidered on it.

It was getting close to rendezvous time when Jeremy told Ellie he had two more stops to make. At a jewelry store, Ellie helped him pick out a moderately priced set of chocolate pearls on a finely braided silver necklace. Then they stopped at a florist for a corsage of baby's breath and a single yellow rose, tipped in red with silver sparkles.

As they waited at the entrance where they were to meet, Ellie looked at him. "Uncle Jeremy, I wanted to say I am sorry for what I did one more time. I wish I wouldn't have done it."

Uncle Jeremy? "Ellie, I have no idea what you are talking about. Something happened last night, but I've forgotten and I have no intention of ever remembering."

Ellie smiled and hugged him once more, very tightly. "Thank you, Uncle Jeremy!"

Everyone else returned from shopping at the same time. Kaitlin saw the hug and jokingly said, "Don't go chasing after another girl while I'm still willing and able!"

Jeremy took a few quick strides before sweeping Kaitlin in his arms, and twirling her around and around while kissing her lips. His kiss left no doubts in her mind whom he loved.

Chapter 23

Kaitlin fussed over her makeup and clothes for two hours. Tonight was going to be special. She wanted to look perfect.

While her preparation took a while, it seemed to take Jeremy all of three minutes to get ready. When she walked down the sweeping staircase, she could hear his deep intake of breath. Then he ran to her, reaching for her hands.

The look of love and admiration swelled her heart.

"Katie, you look exquisite, but words could never fully describe how perfect you are! You don't need makeup, but it really accentuates your gorgeous hazel eyes." He kissed her hand as her face turned ten shades of red.

No one had ever complimented her this way. *Please, don't ever stop!*

"However," he continued, "you are lacking two things."

What? She shot him an angry look. How dare he say that? She'd spent two hours making herself look beautiful. She stomped her foot. "Then tell me, Mr. Perfect. What am I missing?"

His smile was engaging. "Come here. Turn around and close your eyes." There, before the entire Lucia family, he placed a string of pearls around her slender neck.

Kaitlin's hand immediately flew to the jewels as she ran to look in the mirror. The chocolate pearls matched the eye shadow and lipstick she had chosen. "Oh my!" she gasped. "They are lovely!"

By now, Jeremy's reflection was in the mirror behind hers. His arms wrapped around her waist, as he shot her a look that seemed to overflow with love. His voice was only a whisper, "Maybe, but they pale in comparison to you!"

She turned to him and her lips found his. The kiss was long, soft and sweet.

Cassandra cleared her throat and whispered, "Umm... The kids are here, watching, you two."

"Sorry!" Jeremy said, turning to Ellie. "Mind getting the other thing you and I picked out?"

Other thing? *What other thing?* "There's more?" Kaitlin asked.

"Yes, bear with me for a second," he said. Ellie returned from the kitchen with a plastic box. Kaitlin caught a glimpse of the flower. With shaking hands, he pinned it on her dress.

Eyes glistening, Kaitlin saw approval in Cassandra's smile. Ellie looked at them wistfully.

Kaitlin had only worn corsages at her sisters' weddings. She touched its petals. "I have never had one of my own..."

His kiss interrupted her. "I never had the occasion to give one. Tonight will be like our first prom, together."

The night was magical and the romance exceeded any dream Kaitlin ever had. They dined on filet mignon and red skinned potatoes, smothered with buttered mushrooms as well as green beans al dente. Every time she glanced in his direction, his eyes were on her, filled with love and admiration. This was the best night of her life.

The conversation at the table was smooth and pleasant. But the thing Kaitlin would remember forever was the way they floated around the dance floor. Their moves weren't perfect, but the emotions inside were wonderful.

Much before they were ready, the night ended. They took a long walk among the fragrant flowers outside the Lucia's home. Jeremy sang to her, dancing with her in the moonlight, stealing her kisses once more. *Tonight is a fairy tale come true.*

Jeremy held her with her back to his chest, pointing to the North Star. He kissed her cheek and whispered in her ear, "Remember how yesterday, it seemed like everything went impossibly wrong? But we followed our stars and found our way here. I am hopelessly and totally forever in love with you."

She gazed into his electric blue eyes. He always found a way to top even the most romantic moments. Kaitlin turned toward him, finding his lips. She held him close, looking into his eyes that sparkled with starlight. "I'm in love with you, too, Jeremy. Hopelessly."

Quietly, so not to disturb the household, they held hands, sneaking upstairs together. In their room, they helped each other undress. Before he could find clothes to crawl into, she took him to bed, snuggling with him. "I want you to know I love you," she whispered. "I want to make love with you tonight. Will you make love with me?"

Their kisses became more intense as their hands and lips explored each other. Pausing momentarily to catch his breath, he asked, "Are you sure it's okay to make love in your nephew's bed?"

"I wouldn't care if we were in a rocky field filled with poison ivy. Make love to me."

Chapter 24

Early on Sunday morning, Jeremy carried their bags out to the Suburban.

Cassandra held Kaitlin's hand, "So, the big family vacation is in Disney in October. Will both of you be coming?"

Kaitlin smiled, but then her face showed doubt. "I don't know if Jeremy would be ready for that."

"Ready for what, sweetheart?" Jeremy asked as he came around the vehicle. She looked surprised to see him.

"Didn't realize you were here," she replied. "My family holds a kind of reunion each fall. This year, it will be in Disney. Would you like to go?"

Me, being part of this wonderful family? "Of course," he answered quickly, then added with concern, "but only if you want me to."

Kaitlin didn't nod, but the big smile on her face answered that question.

"Let us know the dates and the hotel," Jeremy said. "We'll be there."

Kaitlin laughed and clapped her hands before engulfing him in a bear hug.

Slowly, they said their goodbyes. The thing that filled his heart with gladness was every one of the kids hugged him, calling him Uncle Jeremy. He soon hoped to be their real uncle.

Before leaving, he quietly asked Cassandra for her cell number. "I think something special may happen in front of Cinderella's castle. I might need a co-conspirator to pull it off."

***

The next town on the agenda was above Baton Rouge, Louisiana. It was a long drive across Georgia, Alabama, and Mississippi. About fifty miles out of Louisiana, it started to rain heavily, forcing them to reduce speed. The normal ten and a half hour drive ended up taking over sixteen. They arrived at the motel well after midnight.

The next morning, as soon as Kaitlin climbed out of bed, he was waiting with a tray of food. He loved how she sweetened his coffee with her kisses!

The weather report was calling for a tropical storm to hit late that night. The storm was gaining in intensity coming across the Gulf of Mexico. Instead of meeting at five, they decided to finish up in one day instead of two and meet at seven. The next town would be near Houston, and the short four-hour drive the next day would still give them time to visit NASA.

"I love you, honey," he said when they finally kissed goodbye for the day. Neither really wanted to leave the other, but still, they had a job to do.

Jeremy took the bike, hoping to get done before the fury of the storm landed.

He called her at noon. "Hey, sweetheart! Any update on the storm?"

She hesitated. "Yes. They moved up when it's supposed to make landfall. Baby, let's scrap the extra-long day and we can finish tomorrow. Is that okay with you?"

Ask me to jump off the top of the Eiffel Tower and I would. "Of course, honey. See you back at the motel at five. I love you!"

"Wait! Wanna meet for lunch? There's this really cool sub shop downtown."

"What's up with you and those subs? I'd love to, but we should keep going before the storm hits. We can go out for subs as soon as I get back, okay?"

"I guess, if you trust me to be alone for a couple of hours, missing you and everything," she teased.

"Isn't that why you took the picture of me?" he teased back. "Seriously, let's get done and then we can do anything your heart desires."

"Anything?" she flirted.

"You dream it, we'll do it."

***

Kaitlin was checking out the local mall when the building started to shake. The storm cell had hit with the suddenness of a rushing freight train. It was a little after three-thirty. She reached for her phone. "Honey, is it raining where you are? It's pouring cats and dogs here!"

Jeremy's voice was almost drowned out by the noise of the storm. "Raining isn't the right word. Holy crap! Even Noah would be praying!"

"Where are you? I'll pick you up!"

"No, roads are starting to flood. Meet me at the strip mall on Wellington Drive. I can make it there by four."

"No. Let me pick you up now!"

"It's not safe for you. I'll meet you there in twenty-three minutes. Love you."

The connection closed. As Kaitlin drove to their rendezvous, the rain was coming in sheets, almost sideways. Winds tossed the heavy Suburban like a leaf. Debris was flying everywhere. She slowed to a crawl.

Arriving late, she scanned the lot for Jeremy. He was nowhere to be seen.

She called his cell, but it went directly to voicemail. She left a message as fear started to work its way into her mind.

***

At 3:45, Jeremy couldn't see the road beneath his bicycle tires. Pelting rain blinded him. His jacket had long since been soaked through, and every passing car doused him more. *Be glad to climb into the Suburban and kiss Katie.*

He remembered the road curved ahead next to a rushing stream, but even the solid white line was invisible in the downpour. Crossing a bridge, he saw the water was ready to crest over the roadway. Runoff had multiplied the volume in the stream, raising the height of the creek about four feet from what he had observed only minutes earlier.

Jeremy made a mental note to include this comment in his report.

Above the fury and noise of the storm, a loud rumbling was approaching from behind him. The raindrops glistened in the light from a vehicle. Jeremy braved a quick look, only to be blinded by a wave of water as a big semi roared by. The fender brushed his jacket. Instinctively, Jeremy veered to the right until his pants leg was polishing the guard rail. Suddenly, he heard the airbrakes engage. The semi's brakes were chattering as the driver downshifted to activate the Jake brake. In horror, Jeremy realized the driver was reacting to the curve in the road, making an effort to slow his speed.

He glanced again to his left, now clearly seeing the rivets on the trailer. In that second, Jeremy knew the trailer was going to hit him. There was no room to move farther to the right. His only hope was to jump over the guard rail, but before he could take action, the trailer struck him sharply in the ribs, catapulting him over the rail as if he had been shot out of a cannon.

As if in slow motion, Jeremy could almost count the rain drops he flew past. He estimated his trajectory, moving his arms like wings on a glider to control his landing. A large stone ballast suddenly appeared through the waves of rain assaulting him. He tried to get his arms in front of his face to reduce the impact, but to no avail. His left leg slammed into another stone microseconds before his forehead collided with the five-ton rock.

Jeremy landed face down, out cold in the pouring rain. His cell flew out of his pocket on impact, rapidly sinking in the rushing water less than a foot away. Unbeknownst to him, his bike was now a crumpled pile of steel along the side of the road.

Chapter 25

here are you, baby? Kaitlin was keeping a close watch on the time, calling Jeremy's phone continuously. When he was forty-five minutes late, she couldn't take it anymore. Tears of fear stung her eyes. The big vehicle shimmied from the howling wind as the horizontal rain rendered the wipers useless. And Jeremy was out there somewhere. *God, please don't let anything happen to him!*

In her mind, she already knew. If he was able, Jeremy would have been there. Or at least he would have called.

One thought filled her mind: Jeremy was in serious trouble and he needed her. He had come to her aid when she needed it; it was her turn to help him. She reached for the gear shift. *I'm coming!*

With prayers for his safety on her lips, she slowly eased the vehicle onto the rain-covered road. She began searching for him methodically. Having plotted his last location on her GPS, Kaitlin determined there were only eight roads he could possibly have taken. Lightning flashes lit up the sky, making the airborne debris look like a strobe-lit set from a horror film. The roads were completely empty as she slowly continued her search, looking left, right, and under every canopy or overhang she saw.

She found nothing on the first three roads. Suddenly, the vehicle communication center started pinging, indicating the vehicle only had enough fuel for fifty miles. *What else?*

On the fourth road, water flowing violently across the street at a bridge caused her to halt. The hair on her neck raised as her heart told her to proceed. Jeremy might be right on the other side of the bridge. But Kaitlin knew the dangers of driving through flood waters. How could she forget? Her father had emblazoned the possibilities of losing control, stalling, becoming stranded, or even death by drowning on her soul. Still, something nagged at her to continue. She sat trying to peer across, but the blinding sheets of rain prevented her from seeing anything beyond the raging waters. Mindful of the fuel warning, her hand grasped the lever to shift into reverse.

As she backtracked to cover the other four roads, the nagging feeling drew her mind to the flood-covered bridge. Her worry intensified with the storm. *Please, please be okay, baby! I need you and love you!*

***

The pelting rain and surf coming off the creek filled his nostrils. He exhaled sharply to clear them. "Where am I?" He had no idea, nor did he know how long he had been there. The sheer volume of noise was overwhelming. Something kept stinging his face and head. He had to shield his eyes to protect them. He gazed to his left—a rock strewn slope. To his right, rushing water—was that the ocean? How could it be so close? The waves were inches from his face.

Suddenly, it came back to him. He was on a mission, looking for something. The chopper must have crashed.

He had a duty to find his men and make sure they were safe. Groggily, he tried to raise his head, but the pain from the simple movement almost knocked him out again. Wiping his brow, his hand was covered in blood. His left leg reported in with a sharp pain as soon as he tried to move it. *Where are the others?* He tried to crawl up the slope, but made it less than one foot before passing out from pain.

***

Kaitlin was drawn to the flooded bridge. The wipers were about three speeds too slow to allow decent visibility. Through the tiny sliver they cut in the water on her windshield, she could see the violence of the speeding waters attacking the bridge just ahead. *He's there.* To get there, she would have to cross another low spot in the road. Her father's warnings sounded in her head.

Quickly, she depressed the home button on her cell. When the assistant asked what she wanted, she replied, "Call 911."

"Calling 911." Fifteen seconds passed with no response. She was reaching for the home button when she heard, "I'm sorry I can't do this right now."

"Worthless piece of junk!"

Unlocking her phone, she started dialing the number, but a message across the top of the screen proclaimed, 'No cell service available.' Her cell phone was totally useless.

Her eyes focused to the distant point where her heart told her he was waiting. Separating her from that point was the first flooded bridge. There was no one to help her. Her fingers suddenly hurt. She looked down to see they were white from gripping the wheel so tightly. The depth of the water she needed to drive through to get there was... she didn't have a clue. *Whoever designed roads where you had to drive down to get to a bridge should be shot.* Again, her heart forced her eyes to look at the flooded bridge at the end of the curve ahead.

He needs me. Kaitlin floored the accelerator, propelling the SUV into the rushing creek. The current tried to drag the Suburban along, but she counter-steered, coming up out of the creek. Above the roar of the storm, she heard the sound of something dragging under the bumper. Kaitlin kept moving forward until she reached the top of the small hill, which now looked like a tiny island in the middle of a wide river.

Kaitlin surveyed the area. Nothing—no sign whatsoever of Jeremy. *Where are you?* Her heart had been wrong. Now she had to navigate through the water again to get back to safety. Maybe she had missed him on one of the other roads. Turning left, she started to execute a three-point turn, again hearing something dragging under the chassis. She knew she needed to find out what it was before attacking the flood again.

The driving rain almost took her breath away. She looked under the bumper. To her horror, she found the crushed remains of a crumpled ten-speed. Noting the 'Army Strong' stickers, she knew it was his. *Oh my God! I ran over him!*

Kaitlin dropped to the road, tiny bits of gravel penetrating her bare kneecaps, to see if he was under the car, but he wasn't there. Where was he?

"Jeremy!" she yelled. "Jeremy, where are you?" But her voice was lost in the howling wind.

Looking again at his crumpled bike, Kaitlin's mind tried to piece together what had happened. Hail was now mixing with the rain, but she didn't care. She needed to find Jeremy. A piece of fabric flapping on the guard rail caught her attention. Struggling against the vicious wind, she finally freed it from the joint in the guard rail. Camouflaged vinyl raincoat material, just like Jeremy's...

Her eyes drifted over the rail toward the flooding, raging creek. At first she saw nothing, but when lightning lit up the sky, she caught a glimpse of him, or at least what she could still see. Rushing stream water covered Jeremy past his waist. His arms clung to a large ballast stone.

"Jeremy," she screamed, as she struggled over the guard rail. She lost her balance, cutting her leg and almost smacking her face on the wet rocks. Thank God, she got her arms up in time. The rocks were slippery, so she crawled on all fours to reach him. The sharp edges of the rocks felt like knives stabbing her.

Jeremy's eyes were closed. Despite the constant flushing by the intense storm shower, blood was oozing out of an ugly black gash on his forehead. He was unconscious, yet he clung tightly to a large stone. Kaitlin feared he would loosen his grip and be washed away. She grabbed his shoulder and shook as hard as she could while yelling his name. When he didn't respond, she thought she would lose her mind! Suddenly, his grip loosened and the roiling waters started to pull him away.

She had hold of his raincoat, but the quickness of the water pulled it from her fingers. She managed to grasp his hood just before the waters pulled him completely out of reach, but the velocity of the creek pulled her along. She dropped to her knees, the rocks piercing her skin. Rolling onto her behind, she braced her foot against a boulder and yanked as hard as she could. *God, please help me!*

Her effort gained her maybe six inches. Time and time again, she yanked, slowly dragging him to the guard rail. Somehow she managed to get his limp body over the rail. The floodwaters had risen, reaching almost to the center of the front wheels where the Suburban remained parked on the little hill. Now, she just had to get him into the front seat.

The hail had stopped, but the determination of the storm grew stronger. Raindrops felt like buckshot as they impacted her exposed legs in an almost horizontal approach. Because of the growing depth of the water, she had to change her grip to underneath Jeremy's arms so she could keep his head above water. Arriving at the door, she spun his body around. *I need your help!* To her surprise, an almost superhuman strength filled her arms as she lifted his body into the front seat.

Strapping him in, she touched his skin. It was so cold. He was shivering uncontrollably, almost in spasms. She slammed the door closed. Running to the tailgate, she opened it, rummaging through their bags to grab dry clothes for him. As she returned to his door, she noted the flood waters were multiplying. They were almost to her knees. She removed what she could of his soaked clothes to discover he was bleeding from somewhere on his back, as well as his head. She also saw the left leg of his jeans had dark stains. She feared the stains below his knee were blood.

The intensity of his shivering had grown. She knew he was not only in shock, but was suffering from hypothermia because of the time he had spent in the cold rushing water. Kaitlin covered him with as many dry clothes as she could. As soon as she closed his door, the front of the Suburban started to slide sideways from the force of the rushing water. Holding onto the hood, she worked her way across it toward the driver's door.

She had forgotten about his bike. She tripped over it into the flooded asphalt. Her head went underwater and the force of the swirling water swept her away from the car. Her movement stopped when she struck the guard rail with considerable force. The blow knocked the breath out of her, resulting in a sharp pain in her right shoulder blade. *God, don't let me die. He needs me!*

As she pulled herself up, she saw that the front of the Suburban was also now resting against the guard rail a few feet away. Holding onto the rail, she was able to work her way back to the Suburban. Kaitlin laced her fingers in the grill, stepping over his bike as she shuffled her way around the SUV.

Finally reaching the driver's door, she pulled it open slowly. The rushing flood waters now reached higher than the door jamb. As soon as the door opened, water filled the driver's compartment about an inch deep. It was difficult to close the door.

Twisting the ignition switch, the engine turned over but didn't start. "Come on, please," she coaxed as she tried the ignition again. The engine coughed, but did not start. She tried it again and again until the engine finally roared to life.

There was a loud squealing noise from the motor compartment as the serpentine belt slipped. She shifted the car into reverse and floored it. The vehicle lurched, but really didn't go anywhere. She tried again and again but was making no progress. Banging noises started to sound as large branches and other flotsam propelled by the raging waters impacted the body of the car.

Very little of the small hill was still above water. If she couldn't get them off this slope, she might be able to pull Jeremy out, but where would they go? The flood waters were halfway up to her window and rising rapidly. As her mind filled with fear and confusion, a calming thought entered her head. A quiet voice reminded her this was a four-wheel drive. Searching the dash, she found the button. Depressing it, she again floored the vehicle and kept it floored. The Suburban protested but slowly started to back up in jerky movements.

Over the fury of the storm, she could hear the noise of Jeremy's bike scraping against the macadam, but she didn't care. All that mattered to her was getting him to a hospital.

Keeping the throttle floored, the wheels suddenly took hold and the vehicle accelerated backwards. She wasn't quite ready for this and was soon past the crest of the hill. Turning the wheel to the left, the vehicle violently struck the guard rail. The water wasn't as deep. As she swung around, his bike was freed from the vehicle's undercarriage.

Shifting back into drive, she pulled to the top of the hillock. After a brief but intense prayer, she floored the gas pedal. The intrusion of the SUV into the swollen waters reminded Kaitlin of the splash made when a large ship rolls off the shipyard rails, striking the sea for the first time. Halfway through, she noted the water was almost up to the windshield wipers. She closed her eyes and screamed.

When they opened a few seconds later, she was out of the flood, on soaked roads that were hard to see from the intense rain.

She had one task remaining. Signal lights were out, but she was the only one on the road. Earlier in the day, she had checked out the hospital and she knew how to reach it.

Chapter 26

Kaitlin skidded the Suburban to a stop under the Emergency Room canopy. "Stay with me, Jeremy," she pleaded to his motionless body. She ran inside the hospital to an empty waiting room with no one visible. When she started screaming for help, several staff suddenly appeared. A trail of water followed Kaitlin everywhere she walked.

Two nurses and a security guard rushed out with a stretcher, carefully removing Jeremy's limp body from the passenger seat. He was whisked away, but the guard detained her. "They'll need some information from you at the desk."

The admission clerk seemed to take forever as she obtained insurance and personal information. After finishing, Kaitlin asked to go back. The clerk stated, "Let me get a nurse."

A heavy dark-haired nurse appeared. "Need something?"

"Can I see him?'

"You family?"

A few drops of water made their way out of her bangs to her eyes. She brushed them aside. "I'm his boss. Can I go back?"

The nurse replied, "Only family can go back there."

"You don't understand, I am his girlfriend."

"Boss and now girlfriend? Sorry, family only."

"Dammit! I am his fiancée, the only family he has in the world! Please let me be with him!"

The nurse laughed. "Sure was a quick progression. Honey, you want to see him that bad, follow me."

The uniformed woman led her back to an empty room. "Where is he?" Katilin asked anxiously. She was shivering more from fear than cold, but she was still very cold.

The nurse brought warm blankets and began to wrap them around her.

"It'll be okay. The doctor is evaluating him. He's in critical condition. I don't know any more than that. He was still unconscious when they took him back. Ma'am, are you hurt?"

Like that matters. "No, I'm fine." Now that she was at the hospital, the adrenaline that had fueled her efforts faded. Every injury she sustained hurt, but the pit of her stomach ached over what Jeremy was going through.

She began sobbing while she snuggled down into the now soaked blankets.

It was almost two hours before they wheeled Jeremy's bed back in. His toned body looked so frail and small with tubes connected to his left arm. Several IV bags were hooked up to the tubing. *Jeremy.*

A white-coated doctor came to further examine the patient. "So I understand you are his fiancée," he said, turning to acknowledge her. She could only manage a nod. He offered his hand, "I'm Dr. Sanchez. His condition is critical, but stable." With a few strokes at the computer terminal, he pulled up x-rays on the screen. "He has a severe hematoma on his left leg, a hairline fracture of the fibula, three fractured ribs and inspiration pneumonia." A few more keystrokes brought up the view of his head. "He has another fracture just above his right eye on the skull as well as a severe concussion. He'll need sutures to close the wounds to his leg and forehead."

Kaitlin was sobbing hard now. Through her tears, she got out, "Will he be okay?"

Dr. Sanchez gave her a sympathetic smile. "Yes. That was the bad news. When he wakes up, he will be in significant pain, but he should make a full recovery."

A full recovery? Thank You, Jesus.

"Can you tell me what happened, Ms..."

I don't know. "Jenkins. Kaitlin Jenkins. When will he wake up, Doctor?"

Sanchez pointed to a small IV bag and said, "We'll have to wait and see. We gave him meds to reduce swelling of the brain. These other bags," he pointed to each one in turn, "are saline solution to keep him from dehydration, pain medication, and an antibiotic to prevent infection. We'll be admitting him as soon as a room becomes available, hopefully within an hour or two. He should be alert and oriented by tomorrow. Ms. Jenkins, do you have any dry clothes to change into?"

"Yes, they're out in the car, but I don't want to leave him." She had forgotten how wet she was. She had shivers she was having trouble controlling. From fear or cold?

"I understand that, but he is going to need some TLC. It would be best for you to take care of yourself. You are soaked. While you go get dry clothes and change, I'll suture up his wounds."

Kaitlin kissed Jeremy's hair before she went outside to the car. Upon re-entry, a kind triage nurse took her to a room where she could change. She hadn't realized what a difference dry clothes would make. When a third nurse took her back to Jeremy's room, the doctor was covering the sutured wounds.

Kaitlin pulled up a chair so she could hold Jeremy's hand. The nurse smiled knowingly, dropping the bed rail so Kaitlin could place her head on his chest. In her ear, she could hear his heart beat, strong and rhythmic. She closed her eyes and once again, said a prayer of thanks she had found him.

Staff moved Jeremy to a semi-private room an hour later. Kaitlin refused to leave his side, again assuming the same position of holding his hand while her head rested against his chest.

"Baby, it will be all right. I'm here. You'll wake up soon," she whispered to him. Sometime after one in the morning, she finally fell asleep. The drama of the night before had been worse than the assault against her body. She cared so much. His pain was her pain. *God, if it is possible, let me take his burden.*

It was morning when he began to stir. She felt him move and within less than a second, she was fully awake. "Jeremy, it's all right. I'm holding your hand."

Jeremy moaned and tried to reposition himself in bed.

Kaitlin quickly stood next to him, kissing his forehead. "Baby, I'm here, right here for you!"

His eyes slowly opened until he focused on her face. "Katie, where am I?"

She wiped her cheeks. *Thank You for bringing him through.* "It's okay. You're in a hospital. You got hurt. Remember what happened?"

His eyes focused against the wall. She could tell by his expression that everything was fuzzy in his brain.

"I remember it was raining hard. All of a sudden, a truck appeared next to me. I tried to get out of the way, but couldn't. Last thing I remember was flying through the air before hitting some big stones. Everything after that is fuzzy until an angel appeared, kissing me. How did I get here?"

That was no angel. "I searched for almost two hours before finding you." Kaitlin had to stop to allow herself to calm down before continuing. She told him the rest of the story as she remembered it.

He stared at her in awe, "I guess we're even, huh? I saved you and now you saved me."

Chapter 27

ell service had been restored overnight, so Kaitlin called her boss at the Tower. She was shaking all over, in dread of this conversation.

"I have been worried sick thinking about you," Stange said. "Eighteen inches of rain in twelve hours? Please tell me you're safe!"

"I am now, but there's a problem with Jeremy." *My baby's hurt.* She had to stop for a moment to control her emotions. "He was struck by a tractor trailer and thrown down an embankment."

"What? Where? When did this happen?" Stange implored.

"The doctor said he has a fractured leg, several broken ribs..." Kaitlin thought for a moment to remember exactly, "...a fractured skull, possible punctured lung, and a severe concussion." She told him about rescuing Jeremy.

Kaitlin's pulse was racing. The same icy cold she'd felt the previous night now arced up her spine. Stange could probably tell she hadn't told him everything.

"I'm glad you're okay. What can we do for Jeremy?"

"He's resting at the hospital right now. They said if all goes well, they might discharge him tomorrow, but we'll see."

"What about you?"

How about rewinding the clock so Jeremy wouldn't be hurt? "No, John, I'm all right, a little sore, that's all."

Stange was silent for a moment before continuing, "I hate to bring this up, but if he's hurt that bad, we'll need to replace him immediately."

I knew you would say that. "John, I've been thinking about that."

"What do you suggest?"

"Let's see how quickly he can rebound. I am postponing the visit to Houston."

Stange's voice was subdued. "Why are you postponing Houston?"

She couldn't hide the secret any more. "I love him, John."

The voice on the other end of the line yelled, "What? We must have a bad connection. I'm not sure, but I thought I heard you say—"

"I said I love him. I'll take care of him, see how he does, but I know I have a job to do. I will make a decision by Wednesday of next week. If Jeremy can't go on, maybe you can have a replacement available for the following week." Kaitlin didn't want to consider if she could continue without him. Once again, she fought back tears.

"So this explains a lot, like the discrepancies in room charges on your expense reports. How long has this been going on?"

"For a while. Is it really important to argue about this now?"

Silence. "Guess not. But let's discuss the project. With those injuries, how could he possibly contribute?" Stange said skeptically.

Although she tried not to, a sob escaped as she spoke, "He's pretty remarkable. Let's give him a chance, agreed?"

Stange was quiet for a moment before responding. "Well, based on what you just said, you'd be in the best position to assess this. I know I should keep my manager's hat on and dictate what to do, but I trust you. I know you will be professional, so don't let me down, okay?"

"I won't, John. We'll see how it goes, okay?"

"Realize, we only have about two weeks of buffer left on this job. Jeremy is going to have to be able to perform or we'll need to replace him. If he can't continue, get him back to Chicago. I'll make sure he gets the best treatment possible. But I need *you* to stay on this project. I am hard pressed losing one of you and surely can't afford to lose you both."

"I need to tell you something else. The Suburban is wrecked. I'm sorry."

He sighed, "It's only a car. As long as you're okay, that's all that matters. And Jeremy getting through this, too. Just rent another vehicle. That's why we have insurance. Anything else I can do for you?"

"Thank you, John. Just pray for him," was all she could manage with her tear-stained voice.

For the rest of the day, she finished not only her work, but tried to follow up on Jeremy's portion as well. By the time she got back to the hospital, it was after ten and she was dog tired.

As Kaitlin exited the elevator, she stopped to take a deep breath. Leaving Jeremy earlier in the day had taken something out of her. Yes, she missed him intensely, but seeing such a strong, vibrant man lack the strength and coordination to go to the toilet unassisted was heartbreaking. She was upset, not for herself, but for him. She again stopped her feet at his door, hand softly touching the strong oak wood, reminding herself of the strength Jeremy had inside of him. She sent a brief prayer skyward.

Slowly opening the door, she saw he was out of bed, with an IV tree and tubing attached to his arm. He was seated, staring out the window with a blanket wrapped around him. On the bedside table was a dozen roses, plus a planter. His shoulders were hunched over and his eyes were red.

She hugged him, smothering his face with kisses. "How are you feeling?" He clung to her tightly as he started sobbing softly. "Baby, what's wrong?"

"Sweetheart, I'm so sorry."

She assumed he was talking about his injuries. "About what?" She noticed a tag from GDC on the planter, but there was none on the roses. "Who sent you the flowers? Not been hitting on the nursing staff, I hope."

He shook his head as he stared into her hazel eyes. "I had one of the nurses get them from the Hospitality shop. I wanted to tell you I'm so sorry."

"You couldn't help getting hit by a truck, Jeremy. Just so you know, a lot of people care about you, starting with me." She told him about her conversation with Stange, but left out the part about sending him back to Chicago. She knew something was troubling him, but didn't know what it was.

"I think that knock on my head did some serious damage."

She hugged him, lightly, to avoid pressing on his ribs. "Sweetheart, you took a terrible blow, but the doctor said you would recover fully."

"I-I hope so, but my memory seems to have been affected."

His comment puzzled her. "In what way?"

"The nurses told me I wouldn't be alive if not for you." He squeezed her hand. "They told me I had the best fiancée in the world. I know I do, but..." his eyes pinched together, "...I can't remember proposing to you. I tried so hard, but I can't remember it. I know I planned to, someday. I wanted it to be so special, but I can't remember doing it. This is tearing my heart out."

He wiped his eyes with the blanket, still wrapped around his shoulders.

"You know, I never proposed to Britany. I just said we should get married, and she said, 'Yup.' It wasn't anything special. But when I asked you, I wanted it to be special."

Oh, baby. She let out a sigh of relief. She had expected something much worse, but she couldn't imagine what it might have been. Kaitlin soothed him with a hug, "The reason you can't remember it is because you didn't ask me yet."

"What?" he asked in astonishment.

She knelt so he could see her face. "You see, they weren't going to let me in if I was just your boss or even your girlfriend. I lied and told them I was your fiancée." She kissed his nose.

He burrowed his head against her chest, clinging to her.

"Oh believe me, when you ask, it will be a memory neither of us will ever forget!" she beamed. She held out her left hand, "No ring, no proposal. You see, I'm still on the market!"

His reaction wasn't what she expected. He pushed her away. "On the market, what does that mean? You do know how much I love you, don't you?" His face was filled with fear.

She stepped back so he could see her face fully. "That was a poor attempt at a joke. I've waited my entire life for you and now that you are here, nothing—not even if Luke

Bryan would propose to me—nothing will keep me from being yours and yours alone, forever."

A blush slowly added color to his cheeks, "I didn't know you liked Country music."

"Oh, do you mean he sings, too?" she teased as she stood up.

Jeremy stared at her intently, "Maybe I should do it right now."

Sing? Then she realized what he really meant. Her heart fluttered. *No, please, not like this.* "I-Is this how you want it to be?" she asked as she nuzzled his ear with her lips.

He pushed her back so he could hold both her hands. "No, I want it to be perfect. I want to ask your father's permission first. But I want to marry you, more than anything else in life. Do you want to marry me?"

She knelt down, softly kissing his lips. "Yes, yes, more than anything else, but I will wait—for you and you alone, until eternity passes away if need be." She squeezed his neck tightly.

The sweetness of the embrace surprised both of them. An unexpected sound and flashing light seemed to come out of nowhere, maybe to remind Kaitlin how wonderful their love was. But even more surprising was when three nurses came charging into the room. They forcefully pushed Kaitlin out of the way so they could evaluate him.

The first nurse turned to Kaitlin, holding two connectors on a gray wire, while the charge nurse breathed a sigh of relief.

"You gave us quite a scare, Mr. Roberts! We thought you coded."

"Found the problem, though. The wires to his heart monitor pulled apart. That's what made us think your heart had stopped."

Kaitlin blushed as she stared at the floor. Jeremy smiled weakly, "Well, Katie's kisses always have that effect on me."

Chapter 28

Jeremy clung tightly to Kaitlin as they surveyed the damaged Suburban. "Honey, you went through hell to save me, didn't you? You risked your life for me!"

She smiled and held his hand tightly. "I didn't do anything you wouldn't have done for me."

He quietly laughed.

"What's so funny?" she asked.

He leaned on her tightly as he tried to baby his injured leg. The cane helped, but was awkward. "Oh, I was thinking about how many miles we put on this SUV. I give it to you for one day and it gets all banged up," he teased.

She smacked him in the ribs.

"Ouch!" he grunted in pain.

"Oh, honey," Kaitlin fawned over him apologetically. "I was aiming for your arm, but I missed. Are you okay?"

He grimaced a smile, "Memo to myself, never tease Kaitlin when I have broken ribs."

Moving in for a hug, she accidentally stepped on his left foot. "Sorry! she squealed.

Again, he let out another grunt of pain. "Or a broken leg. Okay, I give up!"

After an apology, accompanied by laughter, Kaitlin helped him into the Suburban and she drove them to the pharmacy. "I'll run your prescription in for you, honey."

"I don't want the oxycodone. Just a large bottle of Ibuprofen. I've had broken ribs before and that's the best cure. Could you please get an Ace wrap for my ribs, some crackers or something, and some water? I can't take the Ibuprofen on an empty stomach."

Kaitlin climbed back into the driver's seat, handing Jeremy the bag. He glanced inside to get the Ibuprofen, noting she had also filled the narcotic prescription.

As she pointed the Suburban back onto the road, she said, "We're going to stay holed up in a motel room for a couple of days and see how you do."

Don't baby me. He shook his head and looked at her beautiful profile. He knew she was trying to protect him, but compared to other injuries he had sustained in life, this was nothing. "No. That will only throw us off schedule. Let's get Houston finished this week."

She gave him a stern look. "Absolutely not. You need to get some rest and recuperation. That's what would be best."

"No. While we're here, let's just do it and get it over with. We're only four hours from Houston."

"Mother knows best, and mother says you need some time off. Starting now."

"You are not my mother!"

She laughed. "Thank God! If I thought you'd do with your mother what you did to me, I'd divorce you!"

Where did that come from? "Hey, you were a willing partner, if I remember correctly!" Then he realized what she said and his face blushed. "We're not married, yet."

"A mere technicality," she said, winking.

Confusion. "Does that mean you will marry me someday?"

"Of course!" Stopped at a light, she leaned across to kiss him. "All you have to do is ask me first." Pulling against her seatbelt, she hugged him tightly again forgetting about his ribs.

"Ow!" he grunted as tears of pain welled in his eyes.

"Oh, I keep forgetting!"

"Not a problem, buttercup. I give in. You win! We'll go to the motel for a couple of days, okay? Please, I can't take this abuse!"

Once back in the motel room, Kaitlin spoiled him, intentionally letting him win a game of Scrabble.

"Baby, why don't you take a dose of your pain killers?"

"No! I saw too many of my buddies get hooked on this stuff overseas. I am not risking it. I'll take my chances and deal with the pain."

She rolled her eyes. "Like that would ever happen to you."

You don't know what happened.

He dropped his gaze away from hers, staring at the floor. "But it did. My first Purple Heart came in Iraq in 2007. We were on a recon patrol when we ran over an IED. It threw me into the side of the Humvee—fractured five ribs. I was the lucky one though, I survived relatively intact. Two of my boys died; another lost both legs that day. I started on the pills they gave me to ease off the pain."

He looked at the bathroom door so she couldn't see the shame in his eyes.

"But even when the rib pain went away, I kept taking them because it eased the other pain. The pain of seeing my men killed and torn apart. I became hooked on them." He paused momentarily. Kaitlin gently held his hand, waiting for him to continue. "When I finally realized what was happening to me, it took weeks to get off. The withdrawal was horrible, but I did it all by myself. I didn't want anything on my service record, so I stuck it out alone."

She kissed his fingers, gently replying. "Jeremy, I'm sorry. I didn't know."

"There are many things I haven't shared with you, yet. Some of the rooms in my mind have heavy doors. In time, I will open every single one of them, to you only. Some of them hide horrible things and those will open slower than others."

As he looked over at her, he saw that her brow was furrowed, possibly in worry, or maybe concern at the darkness of his words.

"But I can promise you this," he continued. "I will share everything with you. Eventually. And don't worry, I'm not an axe murderer or anything."

She smiled. "Like I thought that. What can I do for you?"

I'm so tired.

He reached for her hand. "Can you hold me?"

She climbed in and loosely wrapped herself around him. "Until the day I die."

Chapter 29

*A*s the week progressed, Kaitlin knew Jeremy's pain level had increased instead of decreasing. He told her his headaches were getting worse, too. Not even the maximum dose of Ibuprofen seemed to help him anymore. And no matter what Kaitlin did to help, he couldn't ever seem to get comfortable.

Before the weekend was over, she realized he was in no shape to continue work. The thought of being separated terrified her. How would she be able to make it without him?

But she knew the real question was how would *he* be able to function without her?

While he was sleeping on Sunday afternoon, Kaitlin called her sister Kelly, the nurse. Kelly managed the entire emergency services department for a large hospital in Los Angeles.

Kaitlin reviewed everything she knew about his issues, diagnosis, condition, comments about pain, everything. "Kelly, what should I do?"

"Katie, he needs time to rest, time to recuperate. I'm not so concerned about the leg or rib injuries. They will heal in time. However, that head trauma and the concussion are the most disconcerting. I think he needs to be under the care of a neurologist. Hate to tell you this, sis, but he needs some good old plain rest."

Kaitlin mulled it over, realizing her sister was right. Monday afternoon, she placed the call she'd been dreading.

"John, Jeremy can't continue." She was fighting back tears as she spoke. "I'm sending him back to Chicago. Take care of him for me."

Stange quietly replied, "I will, Kaitlin. Don't worry about that. I'll have Laughman come down on the next plane to continue the project."

It was done. Now she needed to find a way to tell Jeremy.

As they ate their lunch on Tuesday, she broached the subject. Earlier in the morning, he started to talk about going back to Houston to pick up where they left off.

Kaitlin held his hand as she sat on the bed next to him. She stared into those blue eyes she loved so much. "This is the most difficult thing I've ever had to do."

He held her hand and searched her eyes. "I don't like the look on your face. What's going on?"

"We need to talk about Houston. With your injuries, it is going to be hard to accomplish our tasks."

He laughed. "Don't worry about it. I'm tougher than you think. We might have to work a little later every day, but together, we can do anything."

She nodded, finding this conversation harder than she'd imagined. "I have no doubt about that, but I want your total honesty. How are you feeling?"

He was slow responding. "I'm okay. My leg feels good, but I do have a tiny bit of hip and back pain from compensating. The ribs are sore but manageable. Not quite ready for a marathon, but in a week or two..." he slipped her a crooked smile.

"And your head," she asked quietly.

"It's well, like..."

"We promised each other total honesty. Please tell me."

He winced, letting out a sigh. "I hurt pretty badly. The headaches are almost unbearable. But don't worry. I'm fine."

"There lies our problem. I can't allow you to continue," she said as she shook her head.

Jeremy started to protest, but she placed a finger to his lips.

"I need you and want you, and this is harder for me than you," she said tenderly. "I'm sending you back to Chicago. Stange promised me you will be taken care of. When you've recovered, you can rejoin me."

His face turned pale, "No. I can handle it; if I couldn't, I'd tell you. I know my limitations. I can manage this. I want to be with you."

Kaitlin's voice broke as she fought back tears. "I want to be with you, too. I know you can manage it, but I am concerned about your long-term health. As far as you and me, we have our whole lives ahead of us."

Jeremy's breath started coming in rapid clumps. "No! I would rather be with you and be in pain than to be parted from you and pain free. Suppose I refuse?"

She couldn't look him in the face. "I will not allow you to continue to Houston with me. I will leave you here in Louisiana if need be, but I would prefer you go back to Chicago and get better. You slept almost all week and if we were back in the daily grind, you'd be miserable."

He grasped her left hand so hard she thought her fingers would fall off. "Kaitlin, I am an adult and I know my limitations," he pleaded. "Please let me do this. I am a grown man."

"Baby, please don't call me Kaitlin. I am your Katie and always will be. I am doing this because I love you and care about you. I can't let you come with me." She reached into her pocket to pull out a slip of paper. "I

169

booked you a flight back to Chicago. I am putting you on a plane tomorrow. Your replacement will meet me in Houston. It's already in motion." She placed the boarding pass on his lap.

Jeremy stared at the piece of paper for several minutes before turning to look at her. Tears welled in his eyes. "Just like that, Kaitlin? And I have no choice in the matter?"

"Please, I am your Katie! I'm sorry, but you don't have a choice this time. My concern for your wellbeing comes first."

The change in his expression came so rapidly, Kaitlin became scared. His eyes grew wide and wild. His lips pressed together until they were a slight white line. "Bullshit!" he screamed as his anger boiled over. "What it really comes down to is your job, not us. Right? You care more about your damned job than me!"

She recoiled at the ferocity of his words. "No! This is all about you, not about business in any way, shape, or form. The best way for you to get better is to get some rest, away from this project. It's only temporary until you are better. Do you understand? I love you."

"This is wrong," he hissed. "Don't you see how much I need you? I don't think I can survive without you by my side. Can't you understand that?"

Her chin was quivering. "I think I understand that more than you do. Don't think this is going to be easy on me. It's only until you get better, please understand! I want you, all of you, healthy and in good shape, without pain. You are going back to Chicago tomorrow."

"All this time it was only about work." His eyes narrowed and filled with tears. "Understood, boss." With that he stood, pivoted and limped into the bathroom.

***

Jeremy closed the door and sat on the edge of the tub, staring in disbelief.

He heard Kaitlin blow her nose in the next room, then yell, "No, I won't do it!" Then a second later she was pounding on the bathroom door. "Wait! We won't let this come between us; no job is worth this. Let's go back to Chicago together. I'll quit my job. I love you. I won't let you go alone. Please open the door!"

She continued banging, now twisting the knob. He was glad he'd locked it.

"I am going to come back to Chicago with you. Unlock the door, please?"

It took a few seconds for Jeremy to elevate his body from the side of the tub. He stared at his reflection in the mirror before grasping the knob. He yanked.

The door violently swung open. *All that talk about forever. All that talk about how much you love me.* "No, you won't! You aren't coming with me, Kaitlin. You have your precious job to do." *The only thing you really love is your job. We're through!*

She jumped back away from him. "What are you talking about? You can't imagine how much I want to be with you. Stange will have to replace us both. And if he won't, then I'll quit."

His face went red with anger. "No, I won't let you!" he screamed. "You made it perfectly clear your job is more important to you than we are!"

Kaitlin shook her head violently. "That isn't true. Don't be like this. I love you and I know what's important! Just like you once told me, work loses out. Every time. I don't care about my job."

You made your choice, now live with it. "Yes, you do. It's the only thing that's important to you. You go ahead and continue on with this project. I'll be waiting in Chicago when you finish. *Maybe.*"

He hobbled out of the bathroom, pushing past her. Quickly gathering his belongings, he shoved them into his duffel, refusing to even look at her.

"Give me a few minutes, Kaitlin, and I'll be out of your hair."

"Call me Katie, please?"

He turned to face her. "Okay, ma'am. I will call you Katie if you prefer. I'll catch a cab to the airport in the next couple of minutes."

"Your flight isn't until tomorrow. Please stop this! Don't you know how much I love you? Stop this, please! Think of the North Star!"

Yeah, right. His chin was firmly set. "I'm leaving today so I'm not late for my flight home. Even though I didn't ask to be injured, I will follow your wishes, boss." He stormed toward the door, but she blocked him.

Her face contorted in anger "Your boss? Is that all you think of me? This is not my fault. I'm trying to do what's in your best interest! Quit treating me like I'm the bad guy!"

"See what it feels like to sleep by yourself. Maybe then you'll regret 'doing what's in my best interest'!" He could never recall being angrier. His vision started to blur. The world around him started to spin as he grabbed the wall to steady himself. The pounding in his brain was about to make his head explode. He rummaged through his duffel bag, finding the oxycodone. He headed into the bathroom, drawing a glass of water. Without a second thought, he chewed the pills before swallowing.

Kaitlin stared at him. "I thought you didn't want those things! What's wrong with you? Quit acting like an ass and sit down on the bed. I'll give you a massage. That will help you calm down."

Like hell you will! "Keep your hands off me and get out of my way. I'm leaving!' He shoved her out of the way, his body poised in the door frame. "You have your

172

precious work to do. I will not be an imposition to you one second longer!"

Chapter 30

Kaitlin was hysterical. *Damn you! Answer your phone.* After multiple calls it finally dawned on her why her calls were going directly to voicemail. Jeremy had turned off his new phone.

She paced the floor of her lonely motel room, trying to figure out what to do. She didn't even know where he'd gone. Was he at the airport hotel or somewhere else? She needed to talk to someone so she called Cassandra, who answered on the second ring. "How's my baby sister?"

Kaitlin vented incoherently. It took almost ten minutes before Cassandra understood what was wrong. "What should I do, Cassie?"

"Listen, sis. You need to talk to him, face to face. You need to make him understand why you sent him back. You need to make him see this isn't the end. I think that's what he's feeling."

She dabbed her eyes with a tissue. "I tried to. He has it in his mind that my job is more important than he is."

"Is it?" Cassandra blurted.

Are you crazy? How could you even think that? She cursed in anger. "Hell no! I finally found happiness, with Jeremy. I was prepared to spend forever with him, but it all disappeared. I can't live without him. Cassie, I am in love! What should I do?"

Over the next three hours, the two sisters came up with a plan.

Kaitlin's next call was to Stange. Her words were almost incomprehensible. "I sent Jeremy back to Chicago, John, but he's so upset with me! I can't continue without him. I need to come back to Chicago to be with him."

"What? No, no. Wait! Kaitlin, you can't. We need you on this project. It was hard enough replacing Jeremy without losing you, too. I've sent Trent Laughman to meet you in Houston, but your experience and knowledge is what will help us get through this crisis."

She was shaking her head. "John, I can't. I need to be by his side."

"No! I need you there. You can't come back now."

"I'm coming home. Find a replacement for me, please?"

"I can't. You are the best we have. If you leave now, it will fall flat on its face. No one else would understand what you have done. Don't you realize how important it is that we have continuity throughout the entire project? You can't come back until it's finished."

If I do that, I might lose Jeremy for good. "Then I quit, John. He's more important to me than this job."

Stange was silent. "I won't accept your resignation. We have two weeks slack time still built into the project. If you take the time to come back now, you will have to be back on the project every day, with no time off until it's finished. Hopefully, in the next two weeks, Jeremy will be recovered enough to accompany you. Look, Laughman is already on his way down there. You only have three towns left in the southwest. Please, can you finish those three before you come back?"

"John, I can't. I won't!"

The silence was deafening. "I've never asked anything of you, have I?" Stange said quietly.

No, but please don't ask me now.

"I need you, Kaitlin. GDC needs you. If you quit, everything we worked for with this client was in vain. Financially, losing this client and this project will likely bankrupt the company. That client is our future! Please stay with it until you finish those three towns. After you do, you can come back so the two of you can work out your problems. As your friend, I know the two of you are in love. But when you love someone, like I really believe both of you do, you can work through anything. I've been your biggest supporter. Please, I beg of you, please don't let me down. The time apart may actually be good for you. Remember the old adage, *absence makes the heart grow fonder*. Look, if you want, I'll talk to him when he gets back. I will tell him the decision came from me, not you."

Kaitlin fumed silently. John had played the loyalty card. She sniffed, "That isn't true. I won't let you lie for me. I made the decision."

"So what are you going to do?"

Kaitlin hesitated for a few minutes. "I'll stay, but only until we finish those three towns. Then, I am coming back. If Jeremy can't continue, I won't either. Please find someone to replace me because I won't go on without him."

"Then we'll have to make sure he recovers enough to be able to go back on the road. My thoughts and prayers are with you. I know it doesn't seem like it right now, but everything will work out. Everything will be fine, you'll see."

She hung up. Why did love have to be so hard? Kaitlin proceeded to put into action the plan she and Cassandra had come up with. But would it work?

Chapter 31

*T*he painkillers helped a little, but not enough to make any difference. Jeremy was groggy as he stumbled off the jetway at O'Hare Airport. He didn't know if he would have the energy to make it to the cab stand. Clearing security, he headed toward ground transportation. He noted a silver-haired gentleman holding a sign with his name on it. An attractive woman, who looked somewhat familiar, stood by the gentleman's side.

So, Kaitlin had sent GDC to pick him up at the airport. *Thanks, Katie. Thanks for nothing.* He started to skirt past them as he muttered, "I'm through with them, just like I'm through with you."

The woman stepped in front of him. He tried to step aside, but she moved to block him. "Are you Jeremy Roberts?"

She irritated him immensely. "Yeah, and who are you?"

She wasn't smiling, but instead it appeared as if she were studying him intently. "My name is Martina Davis. I am Kaitlin's elder sister."

The silver-haired man stepped over as well, extending his hand. "Jeremy? I'm Stan Jenkins, Katie's father. So glad to meet you! Welcome back to Chicago, son."

Jeremy contemplated not doing it, but he finally took the man's hand. "Nice to meet you. Want something?"

Martina answered, "Yes, as a matter of fact, we do. Kaitlin asked us to meet you. She wanted you to have a friendly face waiting when you deplaned."

The woman was not smiling. *Well, if it was supposed to be a friendly face, why did she send you?*

Stan took his duffel bag without asking. "You look a little pale, son. When's the last time you ate?"

Jeremy's energy was draining quickly. "Yesterday, lunch." He reached for his luggage, but Stan took a step back. Jeremy did not follow.

"Let's remedy that. Come on. We'll take you out to breakfast."

Like hell you will. Your daughter and I are through. "That's nice, but I'm fine."

Stan's smile was engaging. "Yeah, I know, but Katie said you were a Ranger, so I'm sure your sense of honor won't let you disappoint another old Army vet. My daughter wanted to make sure you were taken care of. She sends her love, by the way." Stan studied his face, seemingly looking for a reaction.

Her love? After what she did? Jeremy's face started to contort in rage. "No sir, really. I said I was fine on my own."

Martina replied. "I don't think you are in any shape to refuse. My father is extremely persuasive, and stubborn. The same traits you probably noted in my sister. She wanted to make sure you weren't alone, until she gets back or until you return to her."

Jeremy looked at both of them in shock. *What?* The man had a look on his face as if he had just found a stray dog he wanted to keep. The woman, well, he couldn't read her. *Kaitlin said you were an attorney. Yeah, I can see that.* So she wanted to make sure he was taken care of, huh? Fine! *I'll play along.*

"All right. I'll come."

They took him to a nice Greek restaurant. The food was wonderful. Martina resembled her sister slightly and her voice reminded him of Katie as well. The conversation was pleasant, especially from Stan. They treated him as if he were an old friend.

He was pushing back his empty plate when Stan said, "I'm sorry you got hurt. Katie told me how upset you were when you left. I don't mean to stick my nose into your business, but my daughter is in love with you, son. She only sent you back here so you could get better. I hope you realize that and can understand how hard it was for her to send you away. My wife Nora and I offer our home to you while you are here. Please come and stay with us. You would actually be doing me a favor. Nora loves to spoil everyone and well, you know, with Katie gone, I've been getting spoiled way too much." He patted his stomach. "Nora wants a turn to spoil you a bit."

Despite the food, his head was spinning. "No, I have a perfectly good apartment waiting for me." The disappointment was evident in Stan's face. Jeremy felt a little guilty. "I mean no disrespect. Thanks for the offer."

Martina reached across the table, taking hold of his hand. For the first time, her expression was friendly. "I can imagine how this seems. You're hurt, not only physically, but emotionally. The woman you love sent you away. Then her family appears, wanting to take you in, to help you. A little daunting, perhaps, but know this. My sister wants the best for you. And to her, as well as to all of us, Mom and Dad really are the best. Of course, it's not like being with Katie, but you will be surrounded by love. That's going to be essential for your recovery. Please reconsider. Stay at Mom and Dad's house."

This is all too much. He pulled his hand free. "No. That will not happen. Thanks anyway."

Stan studied his reaction, "We understand. Change your mind, just let me know. Hey, I've got an idea. Why don't you consider coming over tonight for dinner?"

She had set this up. She wanted to make sure he was cared for. His voice was shaky as he asked, "How is she?" After the way he had treated her yesterday, why would she do this?

The two shared a glance. "My sister is pretty upset. She didn't tell us everything that happened between the two of you, but you hurt her badly. Nevertheless, she loves you. Have you looked at your phone today?"

He was having trouble maintaining his composure. *Damned oxycodone!* He regretted taking it. "No, why?"

"She's been trying to get a hold of you since you left. She needs you."

After everything? His heart went out to Katie, alone and hurt by his knee jerk reaction. Tears started to fill his eyes. *I was so cruel to you, yet you won't let go.* He pulled out his phone, powering it up. He realized how hard it must have been to send her family to take care of him. She had tried to call, but in anger, he had turned his phone off. Dozens of text and voice messages instantly appeared on his iPhone. *I am such an ass! You love me, but I was too stupid yesterday to realize it.*

Martina stood, walking to where she could hug him. "It's okay, Jeremy. It's okay. You really should call her, though. We'll take you back to your place now. I had to cancel two court dates to be here because she begged, but we are family. In time, you will see that we always put family first, just like Katie was trying to put you first."

His head started throbbing again as he lost his composure. He couldn't help it. He broke down. Stan also walked around to comfort him. "It's okay, son. Everything will be fine."

They dropped him off at his little apartment. Knowing he had been gone so long, they opened the trunk to reveal several bags of groceries to fill his fridge and cupboards. *So kind, just like Katie.* Jeremy agreed to have dinner with them; Stan told him he would pick him up at five. Stan also volunteered to transport him wherever he needed to go—to work, the doctor's, wherever. All he had to do was ask. Overwhelmed, Jeremy hugged them both as they said goodbye.

I should have expected you would do something like this, Katie. After they left, he listened to her dozens of voicemails and read her texts. After he'd read and listened to every message, he called her.

The phone didn't even have time to ring before her sweet voice filled his ears. "Jeremy. I love you! How are you, baby?"

His voice was breaking as he replied, "I'm sorry about yesterday."

"Forgiven and forgotten."

"I love you. I guess I didn't—"

She interrupted him. "No, it wasn't you. I should have approached it differently. I should have made you understand. I really should have quit and come home with you."

Tears teased his eyes as he immediately realized she had forgiven him. "You did nothing wrong. This was all me. I'm sorry."

She laughed, "Wait! Did you just say you were sorry? How quickly you forget that when you love someone, you never say you are sorry."

For the first time since yesterday, he smiled. "You are right. I love you so much! I apologize."

"Now, that's my man."

They talked the afternoon away until Stan came over to pick him up. Kaitlin told him about the conversation with Stange, letting him know she would be there by the end of the next week. If he wasn't well enough to go on, she wouldn't finish the trip either. She made it plain as day he was what was most important, not her job.

I came so close to throwing this all away.

Stan was right. Nora did love to spoil people and at dinner she spoiled Jeremy immensely. She was a little disappointed he didn't want to stay with them, but she took it in stride. Stan chauffeured him home with plates for breakfast and lunch for tomorrow. The next morning, Stan even arrived to take him to the Tower for a meeting.

Stange ushered him into the office. He got down to business right away. "I know I'm sticking my nose where it doesn't belong, but have you spoken with Kaitlin?"

"Yes sir, I did."

"You two work out your problems?"

He smiled, "Yes sir, we did."

Stange let out a sigh of relief. "Good. I feel better now. Alrighty then, the plan is to get you better as soon as possible. We've set you up with the best docs we could find. I know Kaitlin's father brought you in, but," he handed Jeremy an envelope filled with vouchers, "I don't want you to inconvenience him. These will cover cabs for you for wherever you need to go. Deb Hartwell, our HR Manager, has an appointment set up for you in about an hour. These people are truly the best. They take care of professional and collegiate athletes all the time, helping them recuperate from nasty injuries. I know you want to get back on the job, and of course to Kaitlin, as soon as possible. Follow the course and we'll get you there quickly."

"Thank you, John."

"We're glad to have you with us. Actually, we're thrilled to have both of you on board, for good. Welcome back to Chicago."

Chapter 32

The cab dropped Jeremy off at the rehab complex where they were waiting on him. He was immediately ushered back into an examination room. Within minutes, he was in x-ray, then in imaging for CT scans. The nurse gave him a drink laced with supplements to help his healing. They also injected him with a medication which had an immediate effect of reducing the pounding in his head. He was texting Katie when the door opened.

Before he had a chance to look up, a voice from the past exclaimed, "Jeremy? Is that really you?" He glanced up at the smiling doctor. He recognized her immediately.

He was not smiling as he replied, "Britany? What are you doing here?" She was even more beautiful than he remembered.

"This is where I work. I finished my residency and have been here for six years. This is now my practice. I own this place. How have you been?"

"Fine. Look, I'm not comfortable having you care for me."

"Why? Because we were married once? Because I was a young, stupid girl who divorced you?"

"For starters, yes. Let me make it clear. I do not want you treating me."

She frowned. "I'm sorry, but your employer made it clear they wanted you to have the best available care. That would be me."

Like hell. I'll go somewhere else first. He started to stand. "No dice, Brit. I won't let you treat me. I'm leaving."

She placed her hands in front of her. "I understand and if that's what you want, that's fine. I'll assign someone else to take over the case. But first, I am personally going to exam you, look over the slides and determine the best course of treatment for you. I do this for each and every patient, not just for you. After the exam, I will get out of your hair, agreed? I understand your employer wants to get you back to full health as soon as possible. I am the only one who can do that."

He didn't like it at all. But if this was the gauntlet he had to run to get back to Katie, he would do it. "Okay, let's get it over."

Britany was quite thorough in her exam, coming up with a detailed plan of care involving therapy, medication, and massage. "Is this course of treatment acceptable to you, Mr. Roberts?"

"Yes, uh, Dr... ? I don't even know your last name."

"Roberts. I never married again after our divorce."

"I see. Yes, it is acceptable, Dr. Roberts. You and I are done now, right?"

"Yes, sir. Dr. Peachey will be your attending. I'll go get her." Britany stood to go, hesitating at the door. "For whatever it's worth, I am truly sorry. You turned out to be the only man I ever loved. I'm sorry for the way I treated you."

Sure you are, you miserable excuse for a wife. "You didn't seem to be sorry when you took me to the cleaners. You even took my parents' insurance money."

"Yes, I needed the money to cover medical school. I will bring you a check for every cent I took from you, plus interest."

"I don't want your damned money!"

"Then donate it to someone. I don't want it either. The check will be waiting for you at the receptionist desk. I want to explain one thing you don't know. The problems we had were not your fault. They were mine, even though I wrongly blamed them on you."

Her face screwed up. He thought she might start crying.

"I never told you this," she said, "but I was abused by my cousins when I was a teenager. It took years on a psychiatrist's couch and countless therapy sessions to get past it, but I am cured now. Know what else? I realize now that everything I ever wanted," he saw tears run down her cheeks, "everything I ever wanted, you offered me. I wish I could go back in time and change that. I'm sorry, truly sorry for all that happened." She quickly turned and fled.

He muttered out loud, "Your tears don't affect me, Brit. Katie is my love, everything I want in this life." He shook his head. *I can guarantee you and I will never be together again.*

Dr. Peachey came in, giving him multiple injections to help him mend and ease the pain. Afterwards was therapy, sauna, an ice bath, and a massage. The receptionist handed him a sealed envelope as he checked out, which he opened. It was a check for the money Britany had taken in the divorce. He ripped the check in two, placing it on the counter. He left the clinic feeling much better physically than when he'd arrived.

But seeing Britany again affected him. *What would it have been like if we could have ironed out our differences? Would we have made it this far?* Memories of the good times, all five or six of them, floated in his

187

brain. *Would we have had children? Would we have been happy?* He shuddered at the thought, then murmured out loud, "You stupid idiot! How can you even consider what life would be like after what she did?" His mind drifted to the girl he loved, his Katie. "You were lucky enough to meet Katie! Katie is the woman I want as my wife."

The clinic had called a taxi for him. He hobbled to it and climbed in.

"Where to, bud?"

Jeremy stated his address. As the blocks slid by, his mind wandered. *There is a reason for everything. Why did you come back into my life, Brit?* He pondered that question over and over again. *There has to be a reason. What is it?*

The driver slowed to a stop in front of his apartment building. "Here you go, bud. Fare is twenty-seven even."

Jeremy was digging through his pocket for tip money when his mind put it all together. Everything became crystal clear. "Change of plans. I have something to do before you drop me off. Take me to the nearest jewelry store, pronto!"

Chapter 33

Kaitlin rolled her eyes as Laughman droned on. "So we were drinking our coffee, trying to stay awake during the stake-out. The perp suddenly ran from the building like his pants were on fire."

Life on the road with Trent Laughman turned out to be miserable. A former U.S. Marshall, he had lots of stories. They might have been interesting if not for his monotonous voice. She appreciated what Jeremy had brought to the project. It took Laughman three days to do what Jeremy accomplished in one.

The bright spot in her life was the daily call with Jeremy. She loved how he answered on the first ring with, "Katie! How is the most beautiful woman in the world? Have I told you how much I miss you, adore you, want you, need you, and love you?" Some nights, they talked for five hours. She missed him immensely. For the first time in months, she had to sleep without his arms around her. He kept her up to date with his progress, which seemed to be going extremely well.

The last time they spoke, she asked what he thought of her parents.

"First off, you mom is spoiling me royally. Your dad picks me up every other night for dinner. For the nights

I'm not with them, your mom sends over the most wonderful casseroles. My freezer has enough food to feed a division or two."

She had been so worried her parents wouldn't understand, but they had supported her idea immediately and without question. *Thank You, God, for giving me such wonderful parents.* She wiped her eyes as she realized how much she missed her family. She sent another prayer of thanks the two of them had gotten their problems worked out.

The previous night, Jeremy had spent a lot of time asking about the upcoming family vacation at Walt Disney World. "I can't wait to go there with you! They say it's the happiest place on earth, but to me, wherever you are is the happiest place for me." They had Skyped, with Kaitlin sharing her screen as she walked him through each of the parks online. Together, they created quite an agenda. He surprised her with, "I have a big surprise for you."

He knew how much she loved surprises. "What's that?"

"I booked us an afternoon tea at the Garden View Tea Room at the Grand Floridian as well as a couple's massage at Saratoga Springs."

She inhaled sharply. "Sometimes, I think you really can read my mind. Did you know both of them were on my bucket list?"

His laughter sounded like spring rain. Then came the big surprise. "Honey, when you get back to Chicago, will you move in with me?"

The suddenness of his question floored her. "I-I don't know. Can I think about it?"

There was a little trepidation in his voice. "Sure."

Their call ended shortly afterwards. She pondered his offer. There was nothing more she wanted in life than to be with him, yet she was disappointed he hadn't yet broached the subject of marriage. Her mind wandered. *What will my parents think?* She didn't know what she wanted to do yet. She decided this should be a face to face conversation, not one for Skype.

Laughman was homesick for his wife. Recently re-married to the same woman who had divorced him only two years before, they had a knockdown, drag out fight before the project began. He was originally slated to be the one on the road for this project instead of Kaitlin, but when his marital problems surfaced, the torch had been passed to her.

Kaitlin pondered Laughman's situation as the miles slid by. God always had a way of making things work out. If Laughman had been able to go, she and Jeremy might never have gotten together.

Since both colleagues were in a hurry to get back to Chicago, they worked right through the weekend. Kaitlin had planned to fly home on Friday morning, but because they finished ahead of schedule, she caught the first flight home Thursday morning. She knew Jeremy's schedule, so she planned on surprising him during his therapy appointment.

Chapter 34

aitlin's flight into Chicago landed at eight forty-two. She struggled with her eight bags of luggage, appreciating that Jeremy had always handled this. She finally flagged down a red cap to take care of the pile. Her feet were barely touching the ground. It felt so great to be back in Chicago. *First, I'll sneak home to see Mom and Dad, then I'll surprise Jeremy at his therapy!* Jeremy had told her he would be at the clinic until two. She had a romantic evening planned. As soon as he was done there, she planned to whisk him away.

***

Jeremy had only seen Britany once or twice during his time at the clinic. She was either busy with a patient or else she chose to ignore him. In either case, that was fine with him. He arrived at eight on Thursday morning. The therapy workouts focused on stretching his leg and chest muscles. Alternating sauna and cold whirlpool treatments helped ease the achiness. He could feel his body improving. His mind drifted to Friday, when Katie would return home. He couldn't wait to see her.

Following the whirlpools came a full body massage. Therapy had exhausted him; he was almost asleep when the masseuse entered the room. He was so busy day-dreaming of Katie that he didn't look up at her face.

***

Kaitlin arrived at the clinic with butterflies in her stomach. She had missed him so much, and couldn't wait to hold and kiss him. In her hand she carried a bouquet of roses. Stopping at the desk, she asked if she could stop back and surprise him. The receptionist cleared it with Dr. Peachey before escorting her back to the massage room.

***

The masseuse was a new one for Jeremy. Whoever she was, she had talented hands. As he allowed himself to relax, he noticed the scent of cinnamon and the romantic music of the Righteous Brothers. Strange, he had never noticed either music or aroma-therapy before during his treatments. The combination of the two stimuli brought up a distant memory he couldn't immediately identify. He forced it out of his mind, concentrating on the beauty of Kaitlin's face.

That face slowly melted away as his therapist worked her magic. This girl's hands were warm and soft. It almost seemed as if she knew what to do to make him feel good. He was so relaxed, about to doze off.

In his mind, the hands rubbing his thigh just under the cuff of his briefs belonged to Katie. But when her voice spoke, his entire body stiffened.

"I know you said you didn't want me to treat you," the woman's voice murmured, "but since you came back, I have to tell you that you're all I've thought about."

Jeremy's eyes widened as he whipped around, now sitting on the table. He opened his mouth to speak, but nothing came out. He suddenly remembered where the memory of the music and aroma had come from.

"I want to ask if there is any possibility you will give us another try," the masseuse continued. "You are the only man I ever loved and I still love you. Can we please try one more time?"

His body was paralyzed by shock. Britany seized the moment. She grabbed the back of his neck with one hand while the other gently cupped his cheek. Her warm, soft, strawberry glossed lips touched his gently before opening. Her tongue was tickling his lips. In disgust, he put his hands in front of him to push her away.

***

The receptionist opened the door without knocking. Kaitlin was standing in the hallway but had already taken a step forward into the room. That's when she saw it. Right on the massage table, there was a man and woman ensconced in a passionate embrace. The woman was wearing a white staff coat and had her hands wrapped around his head while his hands were rubbing her... Then it hit her. That's Jeremy!

The receptionist tried to close the door, but Kaitlin shoved her foot between the door and the frame. Using her shoulder, she forced it open. "What's going on here?" she bellowed. "Who the hell are you and why are you kissing Jeremy?"

The woman in the white lab coat turned to face her. "Excuse me! I am Dr. Britany Roberts. Who are you and why have you barged into my treatment room?"

Kaitlin's face paled and her breath quickened. "Britany *Roberts*?" Kaitlin said slowly, turning to Jeremy. "As in Britany, your ex-wife?"

The doctor had her arms crossed as she glared at Kaitlin. "Yes. How dare you barge in here. Who are you?"

Kaitlin looked directly into Jeremy's eyes. "Apparently nobody!" she screamed and threw the roses to the floor. The light pink petals scattered over the dark cherry tongue-in-groove floor boards. The exit door seemed to get farther and farther away with each step she took.

Behind her, she could hear his footfalls as he called for her. "Katie, Katie! Wait, let me explain! It's not what you think!"

You bastard! All this time, she had thought he loved her! Tears blinded her vision by the time she made it to her Toyota. Before she could shove the keys in the ignition, he was at her window, dressed only in his briefs, pounding on it feverishly.

"Wait, please wait! Let me explain!"

"Go to hell, Jeremy. I never want to see you again!"

She started the engine, quickly locking her door. Slamming the gear selector into reverse, she cut the wheel and floored the throttle. At the last moment, Jeremy jumped back to avoid losing his toes. Limping badly, he rushed to her passenger door, trying to yank it open. As she pulled away, he grabbed the spoiler. She floored the accelerator, but when she realized she was dragging him, she slammed on the brakes.

A loud thump resonated through the body of the car. Her eyes flashed to the rearview mirror. Jeremy was no longer in sight. Her head swiveled side to side, searching for him in vain. Finally she decided to pull forward slowly, keeping watch in her rearview with trepidation. Then she saw it. Jeremy's body was motionless on the ground.

How could you cheat on me? Kaitlin's anger slowly started to turn to fear as she watched for any sign of movement. Chills began to climb up her spine as she stared in the side mirror at his chest, willing it to move. Kaitlin whipped around to look out the rearview. Somewhere in the distance, she heard the wail of a police siren. From the corner of her eye, she noted several men running from an adjacent building, making a beeline for Jeremy.

It seemed like it was a good ten minutes, but in reality Kaitlin realized it was much less, maybe thirty seconds before he started to stir. He slowly tried to stand. *I opened my heart and soul to you!*

He fell into a heap. Her concern for him trumped her anger. She rolled down the window and called out, "Jeremy, are you okay?" No response.

Damn you! Slamming the car in park, she placed her hand on the door handle. Before she could pull it toward her, the white-coated slut appeared out of nowhere. Britany wrapped her arms around Jeremy, holding and comforting him.

Once again, anger flooded her heart and soul. Kaitlin slammed the Toyota into drive, standing on the brake while she revved the engine to the max. Finally she removed her foot from the brake, sending a white cloud of rubber toward Jeremy and his ex-wife. She couldn't wait to leave that horrible place.

***

Jeremy felt Britany supporting him on the side of his mending leg, carefully avoiding the still tender ribs. "Are you okay? Who was that woman?" she asked.

"That woman?" Jeremy sighed. "Oh, nobody. Just the love of my life."

Chapter 35

*A*s the sun sank low over the waters of Lake Michigan, Kaitlin sat all alone on an iron bench on Navy Pier. With the heel of her hand, she smeared her eye shadow around her face, wiping mascara on her pants. Sniffling, she pulled the pack of Virginia Slims from her purse. With shaking hands, she lit her first cigarette since her sophomore year in college. The acrid smoke attacked her lungs as she inhaled, immediately resulting in a series of violent coughs. *God, I hate these things.*

One good thing about it, the hacking took her mind off of him. Her coughing slowly subsided. *I'm so stupid. Every time I love someone, I'm the one who gets hurt.* She watched a young couple walk by, hand in hand. *A short time ago, that was us, before he...* She shook her head as they walked away. "I am such a fool. Why in the world did I ever allow him to do this to me?"

Hating the taste of the cigarette, she flicked it into Lake Michigan, only to instinctively light up a second one. *Damn you, Jeremy. I wish I never would have met you!* Fighting back a new outburst, she said out loud, "I wish... I wish you were never born!" Their love had seemed so perfect, like a fairy tale come true. Until today.

She'd wanted to surprise him by returning to Chicago ahead of schedule. The look on Jeremy's face when she walked in certainly did show surprise, but not like she had hoped. *Damn you, Jeremy! You used me, just like every man from my past.* She blew her nose, trying to pull herself back together. *I hate you.*

She was wiping her eyes when a shadow blocked the evening sun. Standing before her was Jeremy, panting hard. His eyes were red. *Tears of regret from getting caught, huh?*

He grimaced in pain as he tried to catch his breath. Kaitlin knew his pain was from the fractures in his leg and ribs. Slowly, he knelt down to look into her eyes. "Katie, I've been searching for you all afternoon. Thank God, I found you. We need to talk. It wasn't what you think. I need to explain. Will you listen to me, please?"

Her hazel eyes blazed with anger. "Are you an idiot, Jeremy? Why would I ever listen to you again? Did you forget about your habit of lying to me, like Geeter being the one who had to tell me you were married, or are you high from the oxycodone? After all I did for you—nursing you back to health, forgiving you after the way you treated me when you left, begging my family to take you in? You're just a self-centered bastard who's only interested in what's in it for you!"

Her fists clenched in rage.

She paused long enough to catch her breath. "You were supposed to be getting better to come back to me. But what do I find? You and your ex-wife making out on the massage table. I'll bet you've slept with her, too! Is that how you repay the love I gave you? I will never forgive you or forget what you did!"

Quickly standing up, she tried to walk away from him. She knew he was going to lie his way out of this to try and win her back. As suspected, Jeremy grabbed her arm, turning her toward him. She wasn't really prepared to see him again, so soon after his betrayal.

His dirty-blond hair was blowing in the breeze. The dazzling brightness of his electric blue eyes revealed pain.

You certainly are a good actor, aren't you? Her vision blurred as she studied his eyes. The same ones she had gazed into for countless hours while she nursed him back to health. The eyes that smiled at her like they did when they made love. Even now, they still sent an electric shock of desire up her spine.

Stop it! I want you out of my life! The problem was, no matter what he had done, she still loved him. She always would, but she needed to get away, right now. *You may be bigger and stronger, but...* She kicked his broken leg as hard as she could.

He yelped, grabbing his wounded leg and pitching forward to the ground.

Towering over him, she yelled, "Are you hurting, Jeremy? Good! Imagine how I felt!"

He grimaced, bracing himself on the bench to stand. Then he reached out to brush the long dark hair from her eyes.

Kaitlin pulled back sharply, anger welling. "How dare you touch me after what you did!" She slapped his face as hard as she could.

He didn't try to stop her.

Pointing a finger at his face she said, "I told you I never wanted to see you again and I meant it!"

Ignoring what she had said, Jeremy tried to pull her close. She struggled, but was no match for his strength. Pulling her body tightly against his, he whispered, "Katie, please! I love you, only you! Please let me explain. At least hear me out."

She struggled, realizing she couldn't break free.

Out of the corner of her eye, she spotted a police officer walking nearby. He appeared to be watching them with concerned interest. "Help me, please!" she screamed. "This man is hurting me and won't let me go! Help! Please help me!"

That did it. The policeman ran over to her aid, grabbing Jeremy by the arm.

Without turning from her, Jeremy slammed an elbow into the man's face, knocking him to the ground, blood spurting from his nose.

Kaitlin pulled free, racing toward the parking lot.

Jeremy started to hobble after her, but a second officer appeared out of nowhere, tackling Jeremy.

She chanced one final glance to see the three of them wrestling on the ground as she fled.

Her hands were shaky as she fumbled through her purse, searching for the car keys. Finally finding them, she started driving. Blended into traffic, she drove around until she found herself at Warbler's Overlook. *He's gone from my life, forever.* She was so sad, she couldn't hold back any more. Kaitlin Jenkins allowed the few remaining tears she'd held in during the day to come out. All alone in the evening dusk.

Everything I wanted, everything I desired is gone. Gone forever. Not knowing what else to do, she drove home to her parents' house. She told them what happened. She had never seen her dad so angry. It was a good thing Jeremy wasn't there.

Nora, though comforting to her youngest, took it differently. "There has to be some mistake. He loves you and you love him."

Kaitlin sadly nodded. "I do. And I thought he loved me, too."

Nora wrapped her arms around Kaitlin. "Come here, baby. Let me hold you while we figure what to do next."

She gazed at the wall vacantly. "He's gone, Mama. It's over."

Nora patted Kaitlin's back, but shook her head. "My heart tells me that isn't true. Is it possible this is just a big mistake?"

Her mother's shirt was wet now. "I wish it was, Mama, I wish it was!"

About eleven o'clock, two uniformed officers knocked at the front door, looking for Kaitlin.

"Kaitlin Jenkins? I'm Officer Brody. We wanted to check on you. Are you all right, ma'am?"

No, I'm not all right. I lost my true love. "Yes, I'm fine."

"Glad to hear that. We arrested Mr. Roberts on two charges. We need to know if you will be pressing additional charges against him."

Kaitlin hesitated, but her father replied, "Damn right, we're pressing charges! What are our options?"

Kaitlin stammered, "N-n-no. I don't want to press charges." *You hurt me badly, but I won't do it. Get out of my life for good and we'll call it even.*

Stan eyed her in disbelief. "What's come over you? After what he did?"

She shook her head. "Not now, Daddy."

Nora appeared behind her daughter, addressing the officer. "How is he?"

Brody's eyes didn't meet Nora's. "Ma'am, he's in the lockup cell downtown. They took him to the hospital for treatment after his arrest, then booked him. He was charged with resisting arrest and aggravated assault. He broke another officer's nose."

Kaitlin's chin quivered. *Hospital? What happened after I left?* "Is he okay? What happened?"

Officer Brody again studied the floor as he responded. "Ma'am, he resisted arrest, violently. The officers had to use justifiable force to restrain him."

I didn't mean for you to get hurt, I only wanted to get away. "How badly is he injured?"

"He'll live. For the next couple of days he may wish he was dead, but he'll live."

Nora's anger was easy for everyone to see. "Justifiable force? Can you explain exactly what justifiable force means? What on earth did you do to him?"

The two officers shared a quick look, but didn't answer. Both touched the brims of their hats as they left. Brody stated, "Good luck to all of you."

After the policemen left, Kaitlin turned to her parents. "I didn't... I didn't mean for him to get hurt. I only wanted him to get away from me. I hope he's okay. I still love him, but... What should I do?"

Nora's embrace was calming, but Kaitlin could feel her mother's pulse racing. Her voice was cold as she replied, "There is only one thing to do, now."

Chapter 36

When the prison lights came on at six on Sunday morning, the brightness almost blinded Jeremy. He covered his eyes with his arm, but the brightness didn't go away. All through the night, lights had flashed even when his eyes were closed. Shortly after waking, four officers came in to shackle his feet and hands, chaining them together. They half dragged, half carried him to the infirmary. Arriving there, he was thrown on a bed and strapped down with heavy restraints. A doctor was waiting, giving him several shots, some for pain and some to keep him sedated.

He was barely conscious when two other officers came back for him at 9:00 A.M. "Okay, Roberts, on your feet. Your attorney is here."

Attorney? He had to focus his thoughts to formulate a response, "I have no attorney."

"Well, you do now. Get up and get your ass moving!"

They forced him to walk to a room with a metal table and two metal chairs. Inside the room, they chained him to a ring in the floor below the table so he had to sit hunched over. His head hurt so badly that he could barely look up. Someone was sitting there, but he couldn't make out who it was. When she spoke, he immediately recognized the voice.

"Oh my God! What did they do to you?"

He tried to smile, "Hey, Martina. Fancy meeting you here."

"What the hell happened to you?"

"Uh-uh. First, tell me how Kaitlin is doing."

There was anger in Martina's voice. "How do you think she is? You destroyed my sister's world. She's home with Mom and Dad, trying to figure out how to rebuild her life."

He had never meant to hurt her. In his mind, he didn't even do anything wrong. *Why won't you hear me out, Katie?* "Then why are you here?"

"Mom insisted. God knows why, but she thinks you're innocent."

"I am. Katie walked in when my ex-wife kissed me. I didn't even know she was there until the door opened."

"Didn't know who was there? Kaitlin or your ex-wife?"

"My ex-wife." The pounding in his head was almost enough to kill him. *Please God, I can't take the pain anymore.*

"So, let me get this straight. You didn't know your ex-wife worked there?"

"No, I knew she worked there. She saw me on the first day. I told her I didn't want her to treat me. She assigned another doctor. I didn't know she was in the massage room. Don't believe me? Call her and ask her yourself." *Not that you would believe another word I ever breathed.*

"Well, Kaitlin is convinced you cheated on her. You broke my sister's heart."

Damn it. I wish this would just end! "I did not cheat on her, no matter what you think!"

Martina studied him for a while before sighing. "Somehow I trust you are telling me the truth. I wish there was a way to corroborate your story so we could show it to Kaitlin; that might help her. Right now she doesn't ever want to see you again. I personally can't blame her, but we'll cross that bridge later. You are charged with resisting arrest and aggravated assault in the first degree. Let's think about what evidence they might have. Maybe there's video of the area, but we'll have to do some investigation."

Martina continued to interview him, taking notes as she came up with a defense strategy. Before she left, she told him that they had a court date at eleven Monday morning, but not to worry about it. As a senior partner in her law firm, she had access to many, many resources, which she planned to put to good use.

The talk exhausted Jeremy. The pounding in his head had increased exponentially.

After Martina left, he realized he could no longer see anything at all, except vague shapes. *God, I can't take this anymore. Take me home.*

Sunday evening was the most unpleasant night of his life. Even the horrors of being wounded in battle—alone behind enemy lines—could never compare to the pain and suffering he was now experiencing. His vision had completely left him. The pain medication they provided did nothing to combat the relentless throbbing in his head. He had even lost his ability to control his bladder and bowels. He didn't know what was happening to him, but he suspected he was dying.

In his mind, Katie's face filled his vision. *Please watch over Katie. I know I won't be around for her anymore, but You will be.* He envisioned a gravesite, his own, with no one else there as he was being buried. He quietly whispered, "Bless my sweetheart. Help her find the happiness she deserves!"

When the officers came at ten on Monday morning to transport him to the courthouse, he was almost completely out of his mind. "Roberts! You didn't touch your food! Putting up some kind of hunger vigil, eh? Get up, asshole. You got a court date in an hour."

He did manage to shuffle to his feet when told, but that was all he could manage. The ride in the prisoner's van was unimaginably horrible. He felt every bump, every sway of the vehicle. He put out of his mind what they were saying to and about him. Nothing really seemed to matter anymore. He felt so horrible; he just wanted it all to end.

At the courthouse, the officers had to drag him into the courtroom. He thought he heard Martina's voice, but he wasn't sure about anything anymore. He knew his life was ending.

Chapter 37

*K*aitlin's parents sat beside her in the courtroom as they dragged him in. Her heart cried out when she saw his condition. "Mom, look at his face!" she said, grasping Nora's arm. "It looks like someone beat him with a sledge hammer!"

With tears in her eyes, Nora held her daughter as they watched the guards seat the man whose face was covered with dark bruises and cuts. Kaitlin started to get up, to run to him, but her parents held her back.

Kaitlin knew Jeremy wouldn't go down without a fight. Martina and a team of lawyers were there to defend him. No attorney was better than Martina.

The bailiff announced the case and the charges against Jeremy. The judge ordered, "Mr. Roberts, please stand. How do you plead?"

Jeremy either didn't hear the request or lacked the energy. His attorneys finally helped him stand up.

The judge repeated, "Mr. Roberts, do you plead guilty or not guilty?"

Martina stated, "Your Honor, before we enter a plea, we would like to ask the court to see video evidence of exactly what occurred on the date in question. After reviewing the content, we will ask that all charges be dropped against Mr. Roberts, immediately. The video surveillance record comes from a nearby restaurant's security camera. The evidence will show that the injury to the officer did occur, but was not intentional. And the record will clearly show the actions of the officer are without a doubt police brutality. If the City exonerates Mr. Roberts of all charges, we agree not to pursue legal action against the CPD or individually against Officer Kurtz. If charges remain against my client, we will go public with the video of this brutal attack on a handcuffed prisoner by a CPD officer. I am sure this footage, which is in my sole possession, will go viral immediately."

The judge glanced at the Assistant D.A., who frowned, but nodded her head. The judge looked at Martina. "I'll allow it."

A large TV screen was moved into place so all could see.

Martina narrated, "The evidence shows Officer Kurtz grabbing Mr. Roberts' arm from behind. Without knowing it was a police officer, Mr. Roberts defended himself. At no point prior to that did the patrolman identify himself to my client that he was a police officer. When Mr. Roberts then attempted to follow Ms. Jenkins, he was tackled by Officer Andrews who also did not make any attempt to identify himself. Only after the ensuing scuffle did Mr. Roberts realize his attackers were police officers. You can clearly see from the footage that as soon as this fact becomes known to him, he raises his hands above his head and surrenders."

The people in the courtroom watched Officer Andrews handcuff Jeremy.

"The defendant is now in restraints, that is, in the protective custody of the Chicago Police Department. Officer Andrews moves off screen to remove the crowd that has formed around the scuffle. We see Officer Kurtz get up off the ground, removing his night stick. From behind, Officer Kurtz viciously delivers five blows to Mr. Roberts' head."

A gasp arose from everyone in the courtroom with each repeated strike. After the fifth blow, Jeremy crumpled to the ground.

Nora squeezed her daughter's hand so hard that Kaitlin thought she would lose circulation. Kaitlin was having trouble controlling her own breath.

"Officer Andrews quickly returns to pull Officer Kurtz away from Mr. Roberts before he can strike again." In the video, bystanders started to fill the area, some reaching out to Mr. Roberts.

Martina paused momentarily. "Officer Andrews' attention is again drawn off to move the crowd away from the victim. As he does, Officer Kurtz can be seen jumping onto Mr. Roberts, now using the end of his nightstick to deliver eight additional blows to the head." Murmurs in the courtroom caused Martina to pause for a few seconds. "Officer Andrews again returns to restrain his partner. Once separated, Andrews turns his attention to Mr. Roberts, turning my client face-up. Officer Kurtz jumps back in, delivering a fourteenth and final blow to Mr. Roberts' face, breaking his nose and knocking out two teeth in the process."

Kaitlin broke down, sobbing hard in her mother's arms as she watched in horror.

"At this point, Officer Andrews grabs and throws Officer Kurtz to the ground. You will note Officer Andrews places his hand on his weapon as he tries to subdue Officer Kurtz. He maintains his hand on his weapon until Kurtz surrenders his night stick to his partner." Martina turned to the Assistant D.A. "I will stop here. The video continues as other officers arrive to disperse the crowd and paramedics place Mr. Roberts on a stretcher. Just before the video ends, one can see Mr. Roberts spit out the remains of his front teeth. I can play that portion if you desire, but I ask you, Ms. Assistant

District Attorney, what on earth possessed Officer Kurtz to attack a suspect so viciously while in restraints?"

The Assistant D.A.'s head was down as she replied, "Officer Kurtz suffered a broken nose and injury to his groin, both at the hands of Mr. Roberts. Kurtz was getting married the following day. They had to postpone their wedding because of the injuries."

Martina's angered eyes opened wide as she spewed, "And that is supposed to justify this brutality? How would you feel if..."

The judge banged his gavel, "That's enough! Order in this courtroom!" He pointed his gavel at Martina. "Ms. Davis, you will restrain yourself in my courtroom or you will be held in contempt. I want both attorneys in my chambers, now. This court is in a fifteen-minute recess!"

Kaitlin tried to go to Jeremy's side, but Nora and Stan held her tightly. Kaitlin could do nothing but wipe her cheeks. Her breathing was shallow and quick. Her stomach felt as if it was going to turn inside out. *How could he do that to Jeremy?*

In less than five minutes, the three returned from chambers. The Assistant D.A.'s face was red, but Martina sported a smile.

They returned to their respective benches and the judge said, "Mr. Roberts, would you please stand?"

When Jeremy did not move, two of his defense attorneys tried to help him. As they did, Jeremy projectile vomited across the desk before falling to the floor. Jeremy's face turned red as his body violently seized. His arms and legs struggled against his restraints. His body rolled on the floor, disrupting everything as he kicked over the defendant's table. The sound of his head and limbs striking the polished floor reverberated through the silent courtroom.

Oh my God! Kaitlin threw off her parents' hands and ran to the front, watching Jeremy fight against his restraints. She screamed at the officers, "Get those chains off of him!"

As soon as they removed the cuffs, Jeremy's arms began to thrash wildly from side to side. The officer who removed the restraints attempted to hold Jeremy still so he wouldn't smash his head against the marble floor.

Kaitlin didn't know what to do. For a few seconds, she watched Jeremy in his suffering. *He needs me.* She leapt into action, trying to kneel next to him. The bailiff ripped Kaitlin from the floor and pulled her back from the scene. Kaitlin screamed, "Jeremy!"

Stan yelled, "Someone call an ambulance, now!"

The seizure lasted almost a full minute before it ended as quickly as it had begun.

Jeremy lay still on the floor, not moving. A uniformed officer moved in to make sure his airway was clear and check for a pulse.

Kaitlin shoved the bailiff away as she pulled from his grasp. She dropped to her knees, wrapping her arms around Jeremy. Kaitlin's face was covered with tears as she held him. "Baby, baby, I'm here. Please talk to me!"

While Jeremy did not respond either to her kisses or her voice, she saw his chest rise and fall in labored breaths.

The ambulance finally arrived, paramedics clearing everyone away, including Kaitlin. Nora wrapped her arms around her, praying softly. The paramedics quickly did an assessment. While one ran an IV line, a second slipped a breathing tube down Jeremy's throat. For a brief second, Jeremy's eyes opened. Kaitlin watched them roll backwards in their sockets.

God, please, please help him.

The paramedics strapped him to a stretcher, applying restraints before starting the IV. Raising the stretcher, they rapidly wheeled him out through the marble corridor.

Kaitlin didn't even ask. She pushed Nora aside and followed, climbing into the ambulance with him, tightly holding his hand. As they slammed the doors closed, Kaitlin whispered to Jeremy, "Don't go. I need you, forever."

Chapter 38

Kaitlin's family gathered around her. After what seemed weeks, a nurse finally came to the waiting room. "Ms. Jenkins?" She nodded and stood. "Mr. Roberts has severe swelling around his brain. The pressure is what caused the seizure. We rushed him to surgery. The surgeon will be able to speak with you afterward."

Kaitlin was inconsolable. *This is all my fault, all my fault!* "Will he be all right?"

The nurse didn't make eye contact, "The doctor will be better able to answer that after the surgery."

God, I know You are listening. Please, please...

Two hours later, the surgeon came out. "Ms. Jenkins?"

Martina and Stan helped her stand, "Yes, sir."

"The surgery was necessary to relieve the pressure from Mr. Roberts' brain. We were able to drill two small burr holes in his skull to evacuate the subdural hematoma, but his injuries are traumatic. We will be moving him to intensive care."

Kaitlin was doing her best to maintain her composure. "Will... will he be all right?"

The surgeon didn't look directly at her. "His condition is guarded. His prognosis is poor. We have induced him into a coma to reduce brain activity. I will be honest, it would be surprising if he survives more than a few hours."

The room suddenly began spinning, going black.

***

The strong smell of ammonia caused her to cough. Not aware how they got there, Kaitlin saw Martina and a nurse on the floor hovering above her. After Kaitlin caught her breath, they helped her stand.

She locked eyes onto the face of the surgeon who was still there with them. In a quiet voice, she asked, "When can we see him?"

The surgeon surveyed the group, frowning, "Hospital policy allows only his immediate family."

Stan stepped forward, firmly stating, "He has no one else. I consider Jeremy my son and we are all his immediate family."

The doctor again surveyed the group, nodding, "I see, but only one family member at a time." He wished them well, again telling them he was sorry he didn't have better news.

Kaitlin was the first to see Jeremy when they finally moved him to intensive care. She couldn't do more than hold his hand and tell him how much she loved him. Seeing him there, apparently asleep, broke her heart. *I'm so sorry. I wish I would have let you tell me your side of the story.* Katie's soul was being torn apart. She wept openly.

A few days passed with no change in Jeremy's condition. Kaitlin's sister Cassandra arrived from Savannah. "Katie, you look like you've aged thirty years. And you're turning into a twig. Go home and eat. I'll sit with Jeremy while you rest."

Kaitlin quickly shook her head, replying, "No. My place is here with him." She refused to leave Jeremy's side. For days unending, she maintained her vigil, resting infrequently in the uncomfortable visitor's chair.

After a week, Cassandra pulled her aside. "Sis, when he comes out of this, he'll need you. If you don't want to eat for yourself, do it for Jeremy."

Kaitlin could tell Cassandra really felt this was all in vain. Even her parents didn't think there was any hope he would ever wake up. And if he did, there was a great likelihood he would have serious brain damage; the doctor had told her parents discreetly—or so he thought—that if Jeremy pulled through, he would probably remain in a vegetative state requiring life sustaining measures for the rest of his life.

***

After two weeks and another follow-up CT scan, the doctor decided it was time to slowly wean Jeremy off the medication that was inducing the coma. Still, three days after that, he remained motionless.

The doctor called for a family conference. "I've been keeping a close watch on his brain activity. It appears to be decreasing." He shook his head as he stared out the window briefly. After wiping the back of his hands across his face, he surveyed the family, eventually turning to face Kaitlin. "I think you need to start preparing for the inevitable. It is doubtful he will recover from the trauma. My advice is that we continue to monitor his conditions and keep him comfortable. With each passing hour, his recovery is less and less likely."

Kaitlin was trying so hard to fight off the tears. "Is... is he in much pain?"

"We really don't know for sure, but I imagine if he would wake up, the pain would be almost unbearable."

Kaitlin couldn't restrain the tears streaming down her face. "How long do you think he will live?"

"I can't answer that. I'm surprised he made it this long."

Inside, her heart toughened. Suddenly, Kaitlin's mind filled with determination. *Oh yes, he will.* She clung tightly to her mother's hand as she yelled at the doctor. "I don't believe you. You're wrong! Jeremy will wake up, I know he will. He knows how much I need him. Get away from me. And get that damned tube out of his throat. He will pull through!" *Please don't leave me, baby. Please don't go.*

After the doctor left, the family sat, discussing Jeremy's prognosis, and his impending death. Finally she could take it no more. Fists balled, she screamed, "He will survive. He will wake up. I have had enough of your negativity. Get out of my sight! Every single one of you. Leave me alone!" She turned, blubbering as she ran to Jeremy's bed where she knew she would be left alone.

Kaitlin sat by Jeremy's side, holding his hand. "Please wake up. I need you." She sobbed and kissed his lips. But Jeremy did not move and there was no difference in the displays on the monitors. Kaitlin no longer left his side, except to use the toilet. She refused to eat or drink, no matter what anyone had suggested. She refused to sleep; if the doctor was right, Kaitlin wanted to spend every second she could with him. *God, please don't take him.*

***

Three days later, her parents and sisters returned, however Kaitlin did not acknowledge them. After an awkward silence, Martina spoke, expressing their concern over her health and mental state. But Kaitlin ignored them. All of her attention was focused on Jeremy. No one else on earth existed to Kaitlin, no one but Jeremy.

She kissed Jeremy's forehead. "Baby, wake up, please. I need you."

A light touch caught her attention. She turned. Her father stood beside her, "Honey, you need to eat and drink or we are going to lose you, too!"

Like I care. "I'm sorry, Daddy, but if he dies, I want to go with him, one way or another. He means everything to me!" She turned her full attention to Jeremy, not noting or caring when her family slowly filed out.

Her mind was steadfast. Kaitlin refused to believe the medical community; she had faith. She believed God would pull him through. *He is my life, Lord. I need him so badly. Can't You see that?*

Every day, she bathed Jeremy, shaving him, never once leaving him alone. She talked to him constantly. "Baby, I'm here. I will always be here. I love you so much!"

The time she spent beside his bed became a living hell. Jeremy would wake, stand and hold his arms open to hold her, but when she stood to hold him, his image would vanish. Kaitlin's mind often drifted. She envisioned Jeremy waking, the two of them walking together through a Disney park, holding a long conversation about their future.

She combed his hair, talking to him. "We will be married in a beautiful garden, full of flowers and butterflies. I can't wait for you to lift my veil and kiss me." Her soliloquy was constant, interspersed only with her prayers for his recovery.

A nurse interrupted Kaitlin's revelry. "Miss, I think it's time for you to eat something. Or at least have some water." She set a sandwich and fresh cup with a lid and straw on the table next to Jeremy's bed, shaking her head as she left the room.

A few minutes later, Kaitlin sat back down, squeezing Jeremy's hand. He squeezed it back almost imperceptibly.

"You know, baby, maybe we should get married in Disney. I'm sure we could find a pastor there somewhere."

The faint pressure of Jeremy's grip hadn't registered.

The barely recognizable voice softly said, "Maybe in front of Cinderella's Castle?"

"That's perfect," Kaitlin replied, adding this detail to the mental picture she was forming. "If only you could wake up."

A few seconds passed. "Maybe you could kiss me so I know this isn't a dream?" Jeremy croaked.

Kaitlin's eyes grew wide. She stood slowly, as though the effort was almost too much. Leaning over Jeremy, she noticed his sallow skin, his eyes still closed. Nothing had changed. Just another hallucination. She pressed her lips to his and kissed him gently, willing the moment to last forever.

As she did, two things happened. Jeremy softly kissed her back, and his right arm wrapped around her waist.

The shock of his touch caused Kaitlin to jump backward. She stood fully erect. Looking into Jeremy's face, she saw his eyes now open, followed by a weak smile.

The room became dark. The vision of Jeremy persisted but she started falling, deeper and deeper into a bottomless black pit.

*** *

Kaitlin's eyes finally opened and she found herself in a hospital bed, her family surrounding her. All of them were smiling. Cassandra hugged her tightly, kissing her cheek. "Sis, it's time for you to come home now. Your work here is done."

Kaitlin understood it was over. *This is it; my life, my hopes and dreams are gone. I know You took him home, God.* She buried her face in her hands. *Tell him I love him. Tell him I will be with him again, someday.* Any possibility of her happiness had vanished, forever. Her body was wracked with sobs. It took her a few minutes to regain her composure. She sadly asked her sister, "When did he die?"

She became confused when each of the family members simply continued to smile at her. Their eyes all drifted from her to her left side. Her eyes began to follow their gazes when the sweetest sound she had ever heard drifted toward her.

"I didn't die, Katie. I heard you tell me how much you needed me. I told you the only way you would ever get rid of me was to tell me to leave, but I am stubborn, just like you. You know how bad I am at listening."

She turned to see Jeremy's tired but happy face.

Kaitlin jumped out of her bed into his arms. Her kisses covered his face as she whispered in his ear, "I knew you wouldn't go!"

He laughed. "Never. I love you too much!"

Epilogue

For Jeremy, it was as if he had entered Heaven. The Saturday of the Disney trip finally arrived. Stan, Nora, Katlin, and Jeremy caught a 7:00 A.M. Boeing 737 out of O'Hare bound for Orlando. Stan had upgraded all four of them to first class. Jeremy snuggled with Kaitlin as he watched her sleep peacefully during the flight.

Arriving in Orlando, Jeremy started to walk toward baggage claim, but she said, "Disney will deliver our bags to our rooms. Didn't you notice the tags we put on our luggage last night?"

"Yes, but I didn't think anything about it."

She smiled, "I keep forgetting, this is your first trip to the Magic Kingdom."

He nodded, "The first since I was twelve."

"You know how much I love the whole princess thing. And the memories we will make together... you will love it!"

Oh, Katie! If you only knew what's coming. The ring box was in his pocket and felt like it weighed 300 pounds. "So, this is where the magic happens, huh?"

She looked at him. He swore he could see her eyes sparkle. "Nope! Anywhere you and I are, that's where the magic truly happens. Oh wait, I almost forgot something!"

"What?"

"This," she said, and Kaitlin gave him the most sensuous kiss he could recall. "That was the first kiss I ever gave you in Florida."

"And hopefully not the last. You've been holding out on me, girl!" His head was spinning from the sweetness.

She kissed him again, "How high can you count?"

She smothered him with many more before Stan finally cleared his throat. "We're going to miss the bus if you two don't quit it! Remember, Jeremy, that's my daughter you are kissing. I know you two are in love, but you're making quite a scene!"

They checked into the Bay Lake Tower resort. They would hook up for supper in Epcot, but for this day, Kaitlin took him to Animal Kingdom. He was totally entranced by the magic of the Disney parks.

They had already set up a photo pass tied into their bracelets, getting their picture taken dozens of times. He loved the 'Kilimanjaro Safari' and 'It's a Bug's Life,' though when they allowed the insects to 'leave first,' he wasn't prepared for it, almost jumping out of his seat.

Kaitlin laughed at him, and Jeremy wrapped his arms around her. "This is the happiest day of my life, Katie," he whispered in her ear. They ate dinner at the Rose and Crown café in Epcot and by this time, Cassandra and John, Kaitlin's other sister Kelly, her husband and their families joined them, along with Stan and Nora.

The first thing her sister Kelly said was, "Let me see your hand, sis."

Kaitlin held out her right hand.

"No, the other one!"

Jeremy glared at her. *Did the entire family know what was coming?*

Kaitlin held out her ringless hand, but Kelly recovered by saying, "I've heard so much about your

Pandora bracelet, I had to see it." When Kaitlin wasn't looking, Kelly winked at Jeremy.

Could it be the secret was still safe?

After dinner, the lovers took a bus to Disney Springs. Kaitlin showed him the Lego shop before they visited the big Disney Store. He bought her an Animal Kingdom Pandora charm for her bracelet and was rewarded with a long, wet kiss. Jeremy, though he knew what her answer would be, was getting nervous.

The next day at lunch, Ellie played the instigator role, challenging Jeremy to a duel to see who could blow the straw paper the farthest in the Prime Time Café dining room. He went first and his waitress saw it.

"I'm telling Mom!" the server hollered.

Before Jeremy knew it, the waitress had him standing up singing 'I'm a little teapot, short and stout.' Cassandra's husband caught the whole thing on video. For the rest of the day, the entire family would start humming the tune and Kaitlin would make him give an encore presentation. Though he acted like it was nothing, he knew this was what being part of a family was like.

After dinner, Kaitlin took him on a bus to the Magic Kingdom. Darkness was starting to fall as she led him down Main Street toward the castle. His heart was in his throat. The ring in his pocket now weighed two tons. *Here's where the magic will happen tomorrow.*

They found a place to sit as they watched the Main Street Electrical parade. Immediately following was the most spectacular fireworks show he had ever seen. He held his Katie tightly in his arms; Jeremy was so full of emotion he could barely hold it all in. He had never known such happiness, holding his girl, knowing that in a short time, he would ask her to marry him and be his wife.

***

Martina and her family arrived late Sunday night. Everyone gathered together in Stan and Nora's suite. To everyone's frivolity, Cassandra's husband played the recording of Jeremy and once again, Kaitlin got him to give an encore presentation.

The big day finally arrived. The entire family headed over to the Character Breakfast at the Beach Club resort. The kids absolutely adored the characters. When Minnie Mouse came to their table, she held Kaitlin's left hand, then pointed to her ring finger, then at Jeremy and shrugged, as if to ask 'Why isn't there a ring here?'

Jeremy simply smiled. *I'll be taking care of that shortly, Miss Minnie!* Jeremy shrugged in reply, but to everyone's surprise, all the women started to tear up.

Kaitlin stared curiously as them. She saw they were all looking at him, so she turned to Jeremy, asking, "What's going on? Is there something you want to say to me?"

Think of something, quick! He cleared his throat, looking at her in a serious manner. "Yes, my love. There is."

It seemed like everyone at the table broke out their cameras, and John started recording again.

Jeremy took Kaitlin's left hand, kissing it softly. "I know they are all crying, but I have to tell you, it's not because of me. I showered today!"

All twenty-four of them practically filled the entire bus for the trip from the Beach Club resort to the Magic Kingdom.

They sauntered together down Main Street, stopping for a family photo in front of the castle. Directly in front of them, while they were discussing where to go next, a show involving ornately costumed princesses began. Kaitlin was totally engrossed.

Behind her back, Jeremy turned to the entire family, holding up the ring box in one hand as he crossed his fingers on the other hand. *It's now or never. Please say yes, Katie.*

Everyone started powering up their cameras again. Nora and Kaitlin's sisters were all smiles. Two of the Disney photographers picked up on what was about to happen and quickly rushed for the best position. John selected a great location for videoing the event.

Jeremy opened the box, dropping to one knee behind Kaitlin. At the climax of the show, fewer and fewer of the people behind Kaitlin were watching the princesses; instead, their full attention was on Jeremy and Kaitlin.

After the bows and applause, Kaitlin was smiling and clapping when she turned around. Before her knelt Jeremy, smiling his crooked smile. Her eyes shifted from his eyes to the box in his hand.

Kaitlin's hand flew to her mouth, and despite the crowd of people, Jeremy felt as if there was no one there but them.

He looked up into her eyes. *Katie, you must be an angel. No mortal woman could be this beautiful.* Though the short time span was only a few seconds, it seemed to last for hours. It ended when Jeremy smiled and began his proposal.

"Kaitlin Elizabeth Jenkins, my Katie, my love. I want you to know that my life really began the moment I met you. The second I first saw you, I knew we were destined to be. All my life, I hoped you, the friend I always desired and the love I dreamed of, would come along. That Friday at the Tower when I first saw your beautiful face, I knew I had finally found everything I wanted and desired in this life."

He had to stop to catch his breath.

"But even though you are the most beautiful girl I ever met, it's not your beauty I fell in love with. Even though your voice is a balm unto my soul, it's not the sound of it I fell in love with. You, my love, just you, in my eyes are the most perfect woman God ever created; you are the girl I fell in love with. I have never been happier. Please bless my life by sharing it as my wife. I beg of you, I can't live without you. You are the love of my life and my princess. Will you marry me, Katie?"

Kaitlin's mouth opened, but no words came out. She simply nodded her head and leapt into Jeremy's arms.

The force of her leap knocked him onto his back. Their lips blended together. Jeremy had no clue where he ended and she began. As their family clapped and cried around them, he neither saw nor heard them. Their kisses were passionate and on their cheeks, tears of joy blended together as one.

Kaitlin stopped to catch her breath, whispering into his ear, "Yes, Jeremy. Yes, I will marry you. I love you so much."

Even the strangers were cheering now.

Kaitlin looked deeply into his eyes before planting the hottest kiss they had ever shared. Jeremy had no breath left in his body. With regrets, he had to break away.

Climbing to his feet, he relished helping his new fiancée to stand.

With her family gathered round, watching intently, Jeremy gently slipped the ring on her finger.

She softly kissed him this time, whispering, "Do you remember the day we met in the Tower—when I was doodling absentmindedly on my tablet?"

Jeremy cocked his head and nodded.

"When I looked down, I was surprised by what I had written. Do you know what I doodled?"

"No, sweetheart, what?"

"Kaitlin Elizabeth Roberts. I want you to know you weren't the only one who felt it right away. I love you, forever!"

Their lips met again as their hearts permanently entwined.

The End

About the Author

Chas Williamson is a life-long Pennsylvanian. Over his life, he has been many things: husband, father, grandfather, amateur historian, as well as a story teller. The desire to write started at a very early age. For years, storytelling was only verbal, but in 2013, a work crisis was looming as his employer of 30-plus years decided to close. His wife encouraged him to use writing as an outlet to reduce stress. When he balked, she asked him to write a short love story. The short love story grew into what would later become *Seeking Forever*. It continued to blossom into three other books of the 'Seeking' series and then a second series. The characters he has created are very real to him, like real life friends and he hopes they become just as real to you.